HAND OVER HIS HEART

THE BRIDES OF PURPLE HEART RANCH BOOK 2

SHANAE JOHNSON

THOSE JOHNSON GIRLS

Edited by Alyssa Breck

Manufactured in the United States of America
First Edition October 2018

 Created with Vellum

CHAPTER ONE

Fran watched the blip on the monitor. It spiked high as though traversing the tallest peak and instantly fell low like a man with a failed parachute. Only to rise and do it again.

If that wasn't a metaphor for his life, he wouldn't know what was.

He watched the EKG monitor as his heart beat a few more times. The pulsing was strong, consistent. For now. But just as the doctor monitoring his heart knew, Fran knew that the beating could stop at any moment.

"Looks like there's no change, Corporal DeMonti." Dr. Nelson's voice was steady, monochromatic like the blipping on the screen he watched. He scribbled notes on a pad with a pencil, looking from one machine, to another, to his watch. Not once at Fran.

Fran was used to being overlooked by those who thought they were superior to him. As a Corporal in the U.S. Army, he'd striven to a higher rank. He'd been a heartbeat away from advancing to Sergeant. Until one mission went terribly wrong.

So, no, the doctor's lack of attentiveness didn't bother him. What did was the fact that the man wrote with a pencil instead of a pen. The graphite touching down on the page was impermanent to Fran. It could be wiped out with the pink eraser on the other end. Just as Fran's life could be wiped out with the wrong move. If the shrapnel that had lodged itself in his chest moved a few millimeters to the left and punctured his heart he would be erased from existence. Gone from the page of life.

"Unfortunately, it's still too dangerous to go in and remove it," said the doctor. He looked up and faced Fran finally. "All we can do is keep up with your therapy and pray."

It always shocked Fran when he heard a doctor prescribe prayer. He would think that most of the scientifically minded men and women would prefer the tangible instead of the spiritual. But he was often wrong. At least he was in the veteran's hospital.

Many of the men and women here had been in and gotten out of situations that could only be attributed to a higher power. So, they didn't shy away from calling on the Lord when their minds couldn't solve a physical problem.

Fran knew full well that his best bet at life was the Lord. So, he had no problem taking the medicine prescribed. He just wished he knew the Lord's plan more clearly. Did He want Fran to come home to him soon? Or was his will to let Fran stay out and play for a while?

Fran preferred having a solid plan. But he also knew the old adage; Man plans and God laughs.

He didn't think God was laughing at him. He wouldn't allow himself to believe that the Creator would make such a cruel joke.

As Fran left the exam room, a few of the women in the halls smiled at him, trying to catch his eye. To the naked eye, Fran looked entirely healthy. He hadn't lost a limb or gained any visible scars, except on his chest. No, his wound was deep. Past the metal in his chest. This wound went down into his soul.

It was all his fault.

Fran and his squad had been doing work to improve the lives of women and children when it happened. The blast that put shrapnel in Fran's chest hadn't taken any lives. But it had taken away six livelihoods, plus the human bomber who'd sacrificed his life for a misguided calling.

For the survivors, their lives were forever changed. And just when they were all getting their lives back on track at the Bellflower Ranch, another bomb had exploded in their lives. No, this couldn't possibly be a joke. It was all too cruel.

Fran pulled out of the vet hospital and headed across town to the ranch. His heart swelled as he looked out at the scenery before him. Montana was simply beautiful.

Fran had grown up in New York City. His mountains had been skyscrapers. His fields had been asphalt. But there was nothing like seeing the beauty and majesty of nature rise up into the sky.

Afghanistan had had the same effect on him. In a place described as a desert, there had been rugged mountains and deep valleys. Snow topped the jagged peaks. The valleys were fertile for crops and livestock.

He'd been shocked to find beauty and bounty in a place portrayed as vile. But that portrait did not include everyone in its frame. The good people of the country tried to keep out of the picture. Very often, they were unsuccessful and the brush stroke of violence colored their lives.

Fran pulled up to the ranch. When his squad leader had purchased the ranch, the soldiers quickly renamed it The Purple Heart Ranch. The lush, violet leaves of a bellflower looked like the emblem of the same name. The Purple Heart was awarded to those who served in combat and were wounded by enemy hands. Each man in his squad had been wounded, and now that they'd come here to heal, they'd been dealt another blow.

Fran and the men of his squad had to get married in a matter of weeks if they all wanted to stay on the ranch that had begun to heal their wounds and had given them back their purposes. The problem was there weren't many women who would want to be shackled for life to a group of wounded warriors. Definitely not one who couldn't give his heart because it could stop beating at any moment.

So, Fran would need to leave the ranch soon. But not before he saw that the rest of the men were settled. Since he'd been responsible for them all losing a part of themselves, he owed them that much. He'd make sure they'd all have the security they deserved. And who knew, maybe they'd even find love.

It was a nice dream. One he'd once had for himself. But it was one he knew he'd never have since his chest was a ticking time bomb.

CHAPTER TWO

*E*va took a deep, steadying breath. Still, her fingers shook. She lifted the pen off the slip of paper, shook out her fingers, and tried again.

She did the math mentally in her head. She couldn't make a mistake writing the numerals and their corresponding amount in words. This was a big check. The biggest she'd ever written in her life.

After triple checking, and then triple checking again, she put the pen down. It rolled away from her, but she let it. She didn't need the ink any longer. The money was spent, and her account was now empty. But it was worth it.

She carefully tore the check from the book. It was check number one. She had never written one before. She'd always paid in cash. This was her first checking account that was used to write and not cash checks. And this was her first check.

She handed it over to the woman behind the counter. Her eyes were kind, and her smile patient. She looked over the check.

Eva held her breath. She couldn't have made a mistake. She couldn't afford another dime to be squeezed into that check.

"Everything looks good, my dear," said the woman.

Eva's shoulders visibly dropped at the confirmation.

"Here's your schedule." The admissions representative handed Eva a half sheet of paper with room numbers, class names, and professors printed in neat lines. "We'll see you on Monday, Ms. Lopez."

"Yes," Eva breathed "Yes, you will."

"Enjoy your classes, sweetheart."

"You, too. I mean, thank you. Enjoy your day."

Eva turned from the admissions window clutching the schedule to her chest. Behind her, the line of students aiming to register was long. They looked bored and tired. None had the excitement in their veins that she had. Likely because most of them had scholarships, or financial aid, or parents to pay for their education.

Not Eva. She'd earned every penny she'd just signed over to the school. It had taken her three years, but she'd done it. She'd saved enough for her first semester of college. Not online. She was going to an actual campus. And not a few community college classes. This was a state university.

She wasn't being a snob. Well, actually she was. For the first time in her life, she was part of the elite class. She just wished her parents could see her now. Somehow, she knew they were looking down on her and beaming with pride.

She'd done it. She'd made her dream come true. Her parents had told her from the first day of kindergarten; education was the key to her dreams. With schooling, anything was possible.

Eva didn't know exactly what she wanted to do with her education. She only knew that she wanted one. She loved being in school, sitting behind a desk while the teacher worked magic on a whiteboard.

These last three years since graduating from high school had been dreary. But soon, she'd be back behind a desk where she belonged. Then, anything was possible.

Eva hopped on the city bus and began the trek home. Home was beyond the nice neighborhoods surrounding the college. Home was beyond the trendy apartment complexes in the business district. Home was a rundown complex in the less than trendy part of town where people worked hourly wages that were often below the state minimum.

The bus didn't get close to her complex. It let Eva off at the church. She'd come to this church a few times in the past few months since she'd been living here. Wherever Eva moved, she always made sure to find a church. Even if she didn't know anyone, church was always home.

"Good afternoon, Ms. Lopez."

Eva turned at the sound of the older man's voice. A smile broke across her face. "Hello, Pastor Patel."

Eva went over and shook the man's hand. He brushed that away and gave her a hearty hug. Eva accepted it gratefully. Pastor Patel gave the kind of hugs her father used to give.

"I haven't seen you for a couple of weeks," Pastor Patel admonished her.

"I picked up a few extra shifts to earn money. But you'll see me now. I'll have more time on the weekends. I've done it. I've enrolled in college."

"Oh, my dear, I'm thrilled for you." He rubbed her shoulder affectionately like her mother always did. "Still, I wish you had taken the church funds."

Eva shook her head. In addition to the need for a good education, Eva's father had also impressed on her that they didn't take charity. They worked for everything that came to them. Give to the church and the less fortunate. For the rest, they relied on family. That was the Lopez way of life.

"Well, now that you're a college woman," said Pastor Patel, "you'll come and give a talk to the youth group tomorrow?"

Eva hesitated. She wasn't sure she had anything to teach anyone yet. She had trouble getting her own siblings to listen to her advice for life. She knew Pastor Patel wouldn't take no for an answer. So, she agreed. With one final hug, he let her go on her way.

Eva walked briskly down the street. It was evident why the bus didn't go into her neighborhood. There was glass on the street. Stench came from some alleys. Men lounged on the street corners in the afternoon before the end of the workday. One of those men was a little too short to be considered a man.

"Carlos," Eva called.

The boy didn't turn, but she knew he heard her.

Eva marched up to her brother. She stopped short of yanking up the pants sagging around his bottom. Where was the belt she'd bought him last month? He turned to her with wary eyes. The guys around him began to snicker.

"I was just hanging with my friends," he said.

"Well, it's time to come and do your homework."

The boys snickered some more.

"Go with your fine sister, little man. When you're done with that school work, I got some real work for you."

Eva cut the thug with her eyes. But the Evil Eye only worked on blood relations.

Carlos came with his sister. She knew she'd embarrassed him. But better those boys think he's a mama's boy or sister's boy. She'd ruin his reputation if it meant he'd be saved from the streets.

"Hanging on the streets won't get you anywhere," she said once they'd crossed the street.

"And school will? Look where it's got you." Carlos raised his hands to indicate the neighborhood. All she could see was various shades of brown, from the buildings to the dirt on the streets to the dirt on the kids' faces.

"This is going to change soon," said Eva. "A college degree is a way out of here. You'll see."

The problem was it would take at least two years to show him the truth of her logic. She just hoped she had that much time to prove her point. In the meantime, she would not let the streets claim her baby brother.

ran parked his truck in front of his place. It was a four-bedroom bungalow nestled in the corner of the land. He'd set up shop here when he'd arrived. He'd been the first to arrive a year ago after they were all discharged. He'd assumed they'd all stay in there, but as the men came to the ranch still suffering from their pains, they each sought out their own space.

Dylan took the two-bedroom cottage next to Fran's. Reed, Sean, and Xavier each settled into the small row houses at the end of the road.

Fran looked up at the place he'd called home for a year. It was a comfortable home, but too big for him. He supposed one of the other guys would move in once they found their brides. Hell, maybe they'd even start families and fill the rooms.

That was yet another dream that Fran wouldn't see come to light. He couldn't fathom bringing a child into this world. Not when he wouldn't be around to care for him, to see her grow, or to leave his wife alone with all of his responsibilities. He wasn't built that way.

He'd have to start packing up soon. But not today. Today, he just needed to check on the other guys and make sure they were on track to matrimony which would secure their stays on the ranch.

The door to Dylan's house opened. Barks and yips spilled over the threshold before any humans did. The first over the threshold was Star, a pug with patches of skin missing from her back. The dog had a tendency to walk sideways, as though she didn't want others to see her imperfections.

On her tail was Stevie, a partially blind Rottweiler with a beautiful grayish-blue coat. The dog kept his nose close to Star to guide his way.

Sugar, the Golden Retriever, made slow work out of the door. His head perked up when he sensed Fran. Fran's spirit lightened at the sight of the dog. Dog and man made their way to each other. From all outer appearances, Sugar looked like a healthy dog.

But the retriever had diabetes which slowed him down from time to time.

Fran bent down and gave the dog's head a good rub. The two had taken to each other the past few weeks the dogs had been there. Diabetes in dogs was rough, but not the end of the line. Maggie, Dylan's wife, took care of all her wounded dogs. Watching her had shown the soldiers that their wounds weren't impediments to love.

"You're back."

Fran looked up to find Dylan coming down the porch steps of his home. He held a dog in his arms. Spin, an Irish Terrier, had lost his hind legs a few weeks ago. Dylan put the dog down and attached a wheelchair apparatus to his hindquarters.

As Dylan straightened, Fran caught sight of the man's own prosthetic leg. It was an unusual sight. Dylan usually kept his legs covered with long pants to hide his injury. But since getting married and finding acceptance for who he was, he'd begun wearing shorts and cargo pants, letting his prosthetic shine.

"How'd it go?" Dylan asked. "What did the doctor say?"

Before Fran could answer, Maggie poked her head out of the door. All of the dogs turned to her, tails wagging and tongues lagging. Dylan turned to her as well. His tongue didn't fall out of his mouth, but his grin spread wide.

"Hon, don't forget Sugar's medicine when you go into town."

Dylan scooped his wife into his arms. He planted a kiss at the space between her cheek and her nose. Maggie smiled into the embrace. Her head turned and her gaze landed on Fran.

Fran had meant to look away, but his eyes soaked up the affection that he would likely never have for himself.

"Fran, you're back," said Maggie. "What did the doctor say? Is there any change?"

This was the other reason why Fran couldn't be in a relationship. Maggie wasn't even his partner, yet she had hope in her eyes. Hope that he'd miraculously be cured. It was an unlikely chance that would ever happen. He was lucky just to be alive.

Fran shook his head and braced himself for their compassion and goodwill efforts.

"I've got a lead on some specialists," said Dylan. "We'll go take a visit."

"I'll keep praying for you," said Maggie. "We're not giving up."

Sugar rubbed up against Fran's side. He leaned down and gave the dog his attention as his friends continued to try in vain to save his life.

"In the meantime," Dylan said, "you need to get looking for a bride. We're running out of time if we all want to stay on the ranch."

Fran hadn't bothered arguing. Dylan outranked him and would have no problem giving orders. Though this was an order Fran would not feel compelled to follow. So, instead, he nodded and changed the direction of the conversation.

"Reed said he was having success finding women through a dating app," he said.

"It's a crazy idea," said Dylan. "But desperate times, desperate measures. Right?"

"I'll catch you guys later." Fran turned to leave. Sugar trailed in his wake. Fran turned back to Maggie. "Is it okay if he tags along?"

"Of course," Maggie smiled. "Just don't let him get too excited. And watch that he doesn't eat anything he's not supposed to."

"I know the drill," Fran assured the dog's owner.

He and the dog took off down the path. The ranch sprawled out around them. He saw Xavier riding one of the therapy horses. The horses helped strengthen limbs lost, but just the feel of being atop a horse gave a man back his sense of power. Fran's day to ride was tomorrow. He wished he could go faster than a trot. But with his condition, he had to be careful.

Instead of riding hard, Fran spent a lot of his time in the gardens. Working the soil was good exercise for the body, but also the mind. Watching things grow under his care soothed his soul.

"Fran, wait up," Reed called out to him.

Reed came from the mess hall of the big house where they ate many of their meals together, even though each bungalow had its own kitchen. Reed waved a phone in his good hand. The sleeve of his shirt was rolled up and pinned to the shoulder of his shirt where the forearm had gone missing, left behind on a blast back in Afghanistan.

"Look at this." Reed shoved a cell phone in front of Fran's nose. "Fifty responses so far."

On the screen was a carousel of images of women. Doctor Patel had told them about the app. It was designed by one of the psychologist's relatives. Patel had a hand in the compatibility algorithm.

"Are these all women who want to meet you?" Fran asked.

"Not just meet me. They want to marry me. And we thought this would be hard." Reed cradled his phone in his palm, swiping left and right with his thumb. Not much slowed the man down or got the man down much less a missing limb.

"Marry you? Complete strangers want to marry you? Do they know about ... you know?"

Reed clicked over to his profile picture. It showed him clearly. He was in uniform with a missing arm. "Only thing a woman loves more than a man in a uniform? A wounded soul she thinks she can heal."

Fran sighed. Not because Reed was being a jerk. Fran knew the man expected to find his true love out of this ordeal. Reed was optimistic to a fault.

"This app matches compatibility to ninety-nine percent. If I can't find my life partner here, then she doesn't exist. I've narrowed it down to these five. This one has a ninety-eight percent match."

Reed held up a picture of a pretty woman. The photo was staged, like she was a model. She was blonde with light green eyes but a touch too much make-up for Fran's liking.

"She's practically perfect," he said. "I've invited her out for drinks this weekend. But she's out of town until the end of the month."

Fran wasn't sure what to say. He wasn't sure if Reed was off his list of soldiers to watch, or if he'd need to keep an even closer eye on the guy to ensure his future was truly set. Fran was determined that all of the men would be settled and able to stay on the ranch after he was gone. Maybe this arranged marriage thing was something, especially if everyone knew what they were getting into beforehand.

Reed continued on, telling Fran more of the woman's attributes. But Fran's attention was elsewhere. Sean Jeffries came down the steps of the medical offices. It was a converted barn they used for Dr. Patel and the nurses and other personnel who attended them and the therapy animals. Sean held the door open, making sure to turn his head so that only his good side was presented to those who came out.

Out came Ruhi Patel, Dr. Patel's daughter. Ruhi was a nurse and often came to help her father with the soldiers that lived on and visited the ranch for their care.

Ruhi and Patel chattered as they came down the steps. Sean looked down at the ground. But Fran saw him sneaking glances at Nurse Ruhi.

Fran sighed. He'd long suspected Sean had a thing for Ruhi. If he did, Sean wouldn't consent to finding a bride on a dating app. That would mean Sean would be leaving the ranch too.

Dr. Patel looked up, spotting the other men. He waved them over.

"I see you're using the app," Patel said to Reed.

"I have a date next week with a seventy-two percent match," said Reed, holding up his phone to showcase a brunette with a round face. Looked like he'd forgotten all about the ninety-eight percent model.

"I think it's criminal what they're forcing you all to do," said Ruhi. "Forcing you to marry to keep your home."

"I thought you believed in arranged marriage," said Reed.

"This is forced marriage. That's illegal."

"No one's forcing us," said Reed. "We don't have to if we don't want to. We can live somewhere else and come here for our treatment."

Sean looked away. Fran knew the man didn't have anywhere else to go which meant there was force in his situation. Fran didn't want to go either. He loved waking up on the ranch. But he didn't have a choice. His heart wouldn't let him stay.

"My father's been trying to match me since I was a teenager," said Ruhi. "I have no interest in arranged marriages. I don't think I ever want to get married. There's no need in this day and age."

The way Sean's throat worked told Fran that the guy was beyond liking Ruhi and was likely full blown in love. This would be a problem.

"What about you, Francisco?" asked Dr. Patel. "Are you in the market for a bride?"

"I can't give my heart away. It's broken."

He'd said it with a smile, hoping to get a laugh. No one did. They all knew his condition.

"It's a cliché, but they say love heals wounds," said Dr. Patel.

Fran wanted to say love couldn't move metal, but he held his tongue and nodded.

"If you're not ready for love, perhaps you can spend some time inspiring the next generation? It's Youth Day tomorrow at the church. I have a feeling your insights, especially your belief in a good education, could enlighten some young souls."

CHAPTER FOUR

*E*va and Carlos climbed the steps to their apartment. It was a three flight walk up. On the ground floor, one of the neighbors had aluminum covering the holes of her screen doors. There were more patches of dirt than grass in what barely passed for a yard.

The heavy glass security door required a key to enter. But as always, it was propped open so that anyone could gain access. Eva didn't bother moving the box from propping up the doorway. She knew that as soon as the door closed shut, someone else would prop something else in the entry.

She climbed the steps with her brother in tow. Bugs skittered out of their way. Off in the corner, a rodent looked up at them as though annoyed that their footfalls had disturbed its peace.

They reached their door and Eva produced a set of keys. She set about unlocking the three sets of bolts before the door gave way, but only a little. The chain link was on.

"Rosalee," Eva called between the chain.

There was a rustling inside. Then the pad of socked feet on the worn wooden floors. Without socks, splinters were an issue.

Brown eyes appeared in the slit of the door. Then it closed. There was a rustle of chain and the door came open, but only wide enough to let the two bodies in. Then a slam and the clanking of all the locks being put back into place.

"You have a good day at school, Rosalee?"

Rosalee shrugged. Her skin was pale. She was lanky instead of plump from her inactivity. Eva knew her sister needed to get out more, or she wouldn't develop better social skills. But inside was safe, so she didn't argue much.

"Got an A on my science paper," said Rosalee, "but a B on my English paper. I'm revising it now to resubmit next week."

Eva nodded. Her sister believed in schoolwork to exclusion of going out and being sociable. Her brother preferred to spend his time outside rather than in the classroom. If she could just merge them together, she'd have the perfect kid.

Carlos went to the fridge. From here, Eva could see it was pretty bare. Things would be hard for a few weeks while she got settled in class. She should be hearing back from the student worker program soon. In the meantime, it would be Ramen every night for a while.

"Aunt Val is in her room with her boyfriend." Rosalee headed back to the room Eva shared with both her younger siblings in the cramped two-bedroom apartment.

Aunt Val had taken them in last year after Uncle Ricardo had his son come back to live with them. Before that, they'd stayed with some distant cousins, but that neighborhood was worse than this one, and Eva had quickly moved them out. Aunt Val's daughter had left the state with her boyfriend, and Eva had jumped on getting her room. Val had lived there for years, which meant there would be some stability.

Giggles and heavy breathing came from her aunt's closed door. Stability was a relative term. Her aunt had a revolving door of men coming and going, but she'd stayed put in that apartment for ten years.

Eva just needed her to stay for two more years, and then she would be able to afford her own place with a college degree and job prospects.

All Eva needed was two years—three tops—before she had her degree secured, a job in the career she chose and moved her family into their own three-bedroom home.

Eva went to the kitchen to prepare the Ramen just as her aunt's bedroom door opened. The burly boyfriend of the week spilled out. He gave Eva a once over that lingered a little too long. Eva kept her gaze averted. She didn't need any trouble with this man.

"Oh, Eva, you're back. I have great news."

Val was in her early forties, but she looked a bit older. She'd had a hard life, raising three kids and losing two of them to the streets.

"You'll never guess." Aunt Val held out her finger. There was a worn, faded-silver band on her fourth finger with a speck of a diamond. One gem was missing. "I'm getting married. Mike proposed. Can you believe it? At my age. I'm getting married."

Eva's hand stilled on the pot she'd just filled with water. "Wow. That's great." Though you couldn't tell from her tone. "So, Mike will be moving in here?"

Mike grimaced. "No. I'm taking my bride and moving her in with me."

Eva gulped. She turned a mutinous glare on her once stable aunt. "You're leaving?"

"Yes, but you can have the apartment all to yourself."

"I can't afford this apartment on my own."

Aunt Val frowned. "Sure you can. Your job pays enough for it."

"I quit, remember. I enrolled in college today. I put all my savings into tuition."

"So? You can do both. You'll figure it out. Oh, Eva. My dreams are coming true."

Her aunt's dreams might be coming true. But Eva's were now dashed. How was she going to pay for this apartment, put food on the table, and go to school? And with the semester starting next week, she couldn't get a refund. She was screwed.

CHAPTER FIVE

*F*ran walked into the room inside the church. It was a Sunday school classroom but the boys and girls inside weren't toddlers. Though they sure were acting like infants.

Boys with sagging pants, even though they wore belts, sat on desks making overtures to young girls who wore more makeup than grown women and small shirts that were meant for five-year-olds.

They were out of their seats or half in their seats. The seats were not in lined up rows. One kid had his shoes unlaced as he swaggered amongst the crowd. The disorder gave Fran a headache.

Even worse, they were all talking over one another. One kid was blaring loud music from his earbuds. That couldn't be safe. This had to stop.

Fran took a deep breath and in his most commanding voice, called the madness to a halt. "Ah-ten-tion!"

All action ceased. All eyes went to him.

"Kindly take your seats."

All of the girls did as they were told, finding seats for their barely covered rumps. About half of the boys followed suit. A few hesitated. One defiantly stood his ground. It was the unlaced kid.

"Who are you to tell us what to do?" The kid swaggered up to Fran. His pants sagged enough to show off his dingy underwear. He stopped short of coming within grasping distance.

Fran closed that distance with two long strides. "Corporal Francisco DeMonti. Are you in the right place, son?"

Though there was no verbal threat in his words, Fran made sure the menace in his voice was loud and clear. He knew he shouldn't get himself this worked up. But his heart rate hadn't increased for fear of this kid. It increased because he saw himself in this kid.

A little punk wanting to prove his manhood, but unsure how. Wanting to puff up his chest, but not having any hairs on his chest yet. Having an increasing ego that could be popped with the wrong prick.

Fran didn't want to deflate the kid. Just bring him down to the size he still needed to be. Not a little kid. Not a grown man. Just a young man.

"Because if you are in the right place," Fran said, "then you might be able to help me out."

The kid chewed at the side of his lip. Fran caught the flicker of relief in the kid's eyes that he wouldn't have to go toe to toe with this bigger man against whom he was obviously outmatched. But still, the kid held his ground, not backing down in the light of authority.

That was unlike Fran in his youth. When a recruiter had come to his high school, Fran recognized the command and took the direction. Not this kid.

"What do you need help with, sir?"

Fran peered over the unlaced kids head to another kid. That kid was notably smaller than the others. Fran couldn't tell if he was younger. There was a mature fire about the kid like those brown eyes had seen more of life than a kid should. But unlike the bigger kids, there was still a light in that kid's gaze.

"I'm supposed to give a speech in this room, but

the chairs are out of order. I was hoping to make a circle so I could see everyone's faces and they could see mine. Do you think you could get everyone to make a circle for me?"

"Sure. I can do that."

Fran stood back while the kid got everyone up and out of their seats to form the circle. It wasn't a perfect circle, but it accomplished what he'd set out to do. With the attention off him, the unlaced kid slunk into a seat between other sagging butts. Once the brown-eyed kid was finished and everyone seated, he turned back to Fran.

"This good?"

"Yeah, this is great. Thanks for that ...?" Fran held out his hand while he waited for the kid to offer up his name.

"Carlos."

"Thanks, Carlos. You've got some leadership skills. That's what I'm here to talk with you all about. Leadership."

Carlos took his seat and gave Fran his attention. The other kids followed suit. Most of them. Unlaced kept his gaze on his shoes.

"Life will eat you up alive if you don't have a plan," Fran began. "Even with a plan, you have to be alert. Don't do anything without honor. Honor brings you loyalty. Loyal people will follow you. I've heard there's been some gang activity in this neighborhood?"

Fran looked around. A few of the boys averted their gazes.

"Isn't a gang like the army?" said Unlaced. "They have a plan. You have to be loyal to get in."

Fran didn't immediately cut the boy off. He nodded, while he thought over the logic. "You make some good points. But dig deeper. What is the plan of the gang?"

"To get money," said another kid. "To protect the neighborhood."

Again, Fran nodded. "But who are the gang members getting money from? Usually, someone who is weaker."

The group of boys, who Fran now noted were wearing the same colors, had no come back for that.

"A real man, or woman, doesn't prey on the weak. In the military, we protect this whole country from those that would try to do us harm. We reach out and help our friends when they are being bullied. That brings honor. To ourselves, to our families, to our community, to our country."

"Are you here to get us to join the military?" asked Carlos.

Fran shrugged. "It's an option. I'm here to make sure you know the difference between someone having your back because of loyalty and someone standing behind you because they're using you."

Carlos's gaze went thoughtful. It was clear he was taking in Fran's words, mulling over their meaning. Meanwhile, the saggy gang huddled in on themselves, closing off anyone on the outside.

That was pretty much the end of Fran's big speech. After a brief silence, he took questions. All anyone wanted to know about was his time in duty, if he'd killed anyone, if he'd fired a gun.

Fran kept the conversation tame. He noted a few of the boys leaning in with keen interest. Carlos was one of those few.

When Fran's time was up, Carlos lingered behind as the others filed out to hear another presentation, or in the case of the gang of boys, leave. Fran's chest swelled with pride that he was able to get through to at least one kid.

"You know what you said in there was nice and all ..." Carlos began.

Fran frowned as he heard the telltale pause of an oncoming *but*.

"But what if the neighborhood you live in is bad?" said Carlos. "And you don't have the money to get out? The only way to keep your family safe just might be by being in a gang."

"There's always another way. Like education."

"You sound like my sister."

"Your sister sounds smart."

"Yeah, she is. But she's still stuck in that neighborhood, too. Her education hasn't gotten us anywhere good so far."

The struggle on the kid's face was clear to see. He wanted to believe, but reality was too harsh. A kid like him would be a prime candidate for the youth program that Fran and Dylan wanted to start on the ranch. Plans on that program had stalled after the edict that everyone get hitched in order to stay. No time like the present to get it moving again.

"Look," Fran fished in his pocket for a card, "I want you to come out to this ranch. We're starting a program that I think you might be interested in."

The kid shook his head and stepped back from the card. "My family doesn't believe in charity. We work for what we get."

"It's not charity. It's work."

He perked up at that. "Paid work?"

Fran considered that for two seconds. They had the funds between Dylan's inheritance, government grants, and their own monthly pensions. Why not? If

Carlos was old enough for a work permit. "Yeah, but there's training you have to go through first. You'll be working with animals. Interested?"

The kid shrugged and lowered his head, but not before Fran saw a light of interest in his eyes. Carlos pocketed the card and headed down the hall in the same direction the little gang had headed.

But Fran was undaunted. Minds didn't change in a matter of minutes. It took time. He'd gotten some of the kids interested in the military. One he was sure he'd corralled. He wanted to get more. He even considered going after the motley crew. He wanted to see the light burn in their eyes as well.

As soon as the thought took root, he dug it up. His leadership days were done. He wouldn't want to have anyone else's life in his hands for the rest of his life.

"It's a great deal of responsibility to have someone else's life in your hands. That's why you have to have a plan."

The voice came as though from an angel over his shoulder. It was soft, but strong and resonant at the same time. It stirred the hairs at the nape of his neck, urging him to turn and find it.

Fran turned, and there she was ...

CHAPTER SIX

"It's a great deal of responsibility to have someone else's life in your hands. That's why you have to have a plan. Education is one of the best paths to a good life."

The words tasted bitter as they came out of Eva's mouth. It wasn't the first time she'd given that speech. It was part of her valedictorian speech back in high school, just three years ago.

And here she was giving it again. In the same slacks and blouse, no less. Nothing had changed about her life. Except for her living situation. That was the only thing that kept changing in her life. Since she was fourteen, there had been no stability in her home life. The only thing she clung to, the only thing that ever gave her anything in return, were her grades.

"Excelling in school, getting a good education, will open doors for you."

A's had opened doors. They got her sent on trips. They got her special privileges. They got her scholarships and awards. They got her recognition. But they couldn't get her family the stability they all required.

An A could get her invited to a fancy dinner, but it wouldn't put food on the table every night. An A could get her a fancy, all-expenses-paid trip, that she couldn't go on without her brother and sister.

"Education can lessen the challenges you'll face in life."

When Eva was a high school senior on the stage, the speech hadn't included qualifying words like *can* and *might*. She'd gone into her speech making full, declarative statements. Not any longer.

"Knowledge can lead to more opportunities that might enhance your personal life and could enhance your career."

She looked out at the book-smart girls, wondering how many would end up in dead-end jobs. How many would have to take out loans for their education, and then work to pay it back for the rest of their lives? Because that's the life she was looking at now. And that was only if she could get a loan.

She had no collateral. She didn't have bad credit. It was worse. She had no credit. It was unlikely anyone would loan her some advice. And she could only get half her money back from the college with classes starting in a couple of days.

She was screwed. But she didn't know what else to tell these kids. Go into a life of crime? No, that would end their lives sooner. Get married and depend on your spouse? And take a big step back in the women's movement.

She took a step back from the lectern in the small classroom. When she did, she spied someone in the doorway who wasn't a kid. He was definitely all man. And he was staring at her, gazing at her. Could he see she was a fraud?

Despite everything, she'd been through, and all of her setbacks, Eva knew that what she was telling these kids was the only solution, the only chance these kids had. And so she went on.

"Life doesn't always work out the way you plan," she said. "But what does? You can't give up because you will get knocked down. That's just one more check off the list of the wrong way to go. You'll get there eventually. If you just don't give up."

She'd told herself right then and there that she wouldn't give up. No matter how long it took, she'd get her degree. She'd get her family into a good financial and living situation. It was just going to take even longer than she'd planned. But it was her plan.

The end of her speech was met with polite applause. The kids got up and filed out of the room in haste. Eva preferred to think it was due to the snacks being served in the hall and not her lackluster speech. She pinched the bridge between her nose and forehead, then gathered her belongings, and made for the door. A broad chest blocked her path.

Eva looked up into the eyes of the man who'd been standing at the door. He gazed down at her with a smile. She felt that he saw right through her.

"I'm sorry," she said.

"What for?"

"What I said. I must've sounded like an idiot."

"I loved what you said."

"You loved it?"

"Yeah, your words. I agree with you. Education, having a plan, those are the keys to success."

"It didn't work for me," she admitted. "I got all A's. I got a full scholarship. But I wasn't able to go to school."

She had no idea why she was spilling her soul to this guy. Something about his face made her trust him, let her know that she was safe. Her gaze slid back down to his chest. She wondered what kind of hugs he gave. She bet they were strong and secure.

"What's holding you back?"

"Pardon?" She felt her cheeks flaming. Had he heard her thoughts?

"Why haven't you gone to college?"

"My parents died. My dad died in an accident. My mom died of cancer."

"I'm sorry."

"I have two younger siblings. I've had to take care of them. Couldn't do that while going to college at the same time. I know some people do it. But I had to work to pay the bills and put food on the table."

"There was no one else in your family to help?"

She took a deep breath, trying to determine how to keep this story short. She didn't want to go into it. He seemed to sense that. Something in his eyes, in his wry smile, told her that she didn't have to tell him anything. Which made her want to tell him everything.

43

"I didn't give up," she said. "I made a new plan. It was going to work. I was so close. But it fell apart."

"What's happened?"

"I have to drop out. Again. I had to give up my scholarship the first time because the relative I trusted to take care of my siblings didn't. I came home to work and care for them. I saved every penny I could over the last three years. I was ready to go back. But now the new relative we're staying with has let us down again. I already paid for the semester, and I can't get all of my money back. It's a mess."

The words all came out in a blubbering mush. Tears streamed down Eva's cheeks.

And then she was enveloped in a hug. A strong heartbeat next to her ear. It was the best hug of the century. Warm, fluffy in the center. Firm at the edges. And did she mention warm? She wanted to stay forever.

But she couldn't. This guy was a stranger, and she was blubbering all over him. Eva pulled herself together and away from him.

"It's okay." She was soothing him, more than she was soothing herself. "I have a new plan. Or at least I will. I just have to get my family straight first."

"You mean, Carlos."

"You know my brother."

He nodded, gazing directly into her eyes. Her breath caught as he held her there with only his eyes. He wasn't touching her any longer. Just looking at her without pity, only compassion and certainty.

"I want to help," he said. "There's a ranch for troubled kids—"

"My brother's not troubled."

"Not yet. He wants to do good, I see it in him. But he's eyeing the wrong path. This could help set him on the right path. I ..."

His words trailed away. His—she didn't even know his name. Whoever he was, his gaze was beyond her. Out the window.

Eva turned and saw a group of boys. She recognized them as members of the neighborhood gang. And standing in the midst of them, being shoved around, was her brother.

CHAPTER SEVEN

*T*he scene out the window came slowly into focus. The group of boys encircling one didn't hold Fran's full attention at first. The woman encircled in his arms did.

She smelled of a gentle summer breeze mixed with a hint of soap and the spicy noodles he used to eat in college. He had the urge to put his nose just behind her ear and inhale. It had been so long since he'd held someone.

She was all soft curves and warm heat. She was small and vulnerable, but there was still a strength in the way her back didn't bend as she leaned into him.

When her head came to rest against his heart, it didn't skip a beat. It stopped. One second it thumped rhythmically. In the next, it stood still, as though sensing something big, something important. Not danger, but something life-altering just the same.

When it started up again, it went from zero to sixty. The pounding made Fran's breath catch, which in turn brought more of her scent into his nose.

Down her scent went, over his tongue, down his throat, past his heart, and into his gut. It rocked him back onto his heels. Her fingers clenched where they rested on his lower back. It brought her chest into his, which made his heart beat even faster.

This was not good for his wounded heart. He had to let this girl go. But how could he when she was in distress. If this hug helped her, it was the least he could do. Right?

He couldn't do anything about her unreliable family, or the tragic death of her parents. But he could do something about her brother. Which brought his attention back to the window where Carlos was being surrounded by the group of boys from the talk.

Fran went to tell Carlos's sister only to look down and find that she was no longer in his arms. She was already headed for the exit. Fran kicked himself into gear to go after her.

He caught up to her just as she pushed the church doors open and stepped outside.

"Oh, look, here comes your sister."

"Get away from him," she said.

The boys were all younger than her, but they all had at least a foot on her. Didn't appear to deter the little scholar. She marched right up to them with her head thrown back and her hands on her hips. It would've cowed Fran. Unfortunately, these boys weren't as smart as he was.

"Or what?" said the kid with the unlaced shoes. "This has nothing to do with you." The boy raised his hand and shoved the woman's shoulder.

But before the kid could make contact, or Fran could rip his arm off, Carlos was there, shoving the boy's hand aside. "Don't you dare put your hands on my sister."

"Or what? You ain't got nobody but women to protect you. You should've joined us when you had the chance."

Behind the boys, someone cleared their throat. They all looked over to Fran. Fran towered over everyone before him.

"What are you gonna do, soldier boy?" But there was a tremor in the kid's voice.

"I'm going to ask real nice and hope that you have the brains to listen."

The kid snorted, showing he had no brains. "There's four of us and one of you."

"Yeah, pretty unfair odds."

Fran reached out and grabbed the boy's hand, the one that had almost touched the woman. With a flick of his wrist, Fran tweaked the boy's joint. The kid dropped like a sack to his knees. His eyes teared up.

Fran caught movement out of the corner of his eye. He turned to face the other three boys. They'd been moving in. They hesitated now. With the glare Fran gave them, they each took a step back.

"Apologize to the lady." Fran's voice was a low growl. His heartbeat was steady now. These punks he could handle. He would not countenance any of them harming a woman, especially this woman who'd felt like a sunbeam caught in his arms.

"What? Fu-ahhhhhh!"

Fran tweaked the kid's arm more, sending his chest into the ground while his arm stuck out at an unnatural angle behind his back. His boys made to move. Fran lifted a brow at them. That was all it took for them to back down.

"Sorry, sorry, Eva. Sorry," the boy sang like a canary.

Fran loosened his grip, not gently so that the pain would ebb. No, he let the joints crack. The kid crab walked his way to his friends. His eyes glowed with fear, but his chest rose and fell with sore pride. His gaze jerked from Fran and found Carlos.

"Watch your back, you little punk," the kid said as he scrambled to his feet.

Eva stepped in front of her brother, a menacing look on her pretty face. Fran's heart skipped at the sight of her fierceness.

"Why did you step in?" said Carlos, turning on his sister once they were gone. "Now everyone will think I'm a mama's boy."

"Would you have rather I let them push you around and beat you up?" Eva demanded.

"At least that would prove that I'm a man."

"No," said Fran. "That wouldn't prove you're a man. Standing up for your sister when that punk came at her proved it. The fact that they came at you in numbers proved they're not men at all."

"But you have a unit," said Carlos.

Fran nodded. "My brothers would have my back. But they'd stay at my back and keep out of it if the fight was fair. That was not a fair fight. There was no honor in those boys. You did good."

"Come on, Carlos, let's get home," said Eva. "The bus will be here soon."

"I can take you," said Fran. "My truck is just out front."

Eva looked him up and down. Just a moment ago he'd held her in his arms while she let her guard down. Now her shields were up.

"Please," he said. "I'd like to make sure you two got home safe. Those kids might still be lying in wait."

"They'll be lying in wait tomorrow," said Carlos. "Or the next day."

Eva's face contorted. Fran wanted to wipe the look away and soothe her worries. For now, he could offer them a ride home and offer to take Carlos under his wing at the ranch.

Eva went inside to get her things. Then they all piled into his truck. Carlos in the passenger seat, Eva in the back seat. Fran didn't like her so far out of his reach. But it was for the best.

He drove them about two miles down the road into a part of the town he hadn't been before. There was trash on the sidewalks. It was run down with men hanging on the street corners. The way their eyes followed his car reminded him of the locals in the war zone, hungry and desperate for a way out.

Eva remained quiet in the back seat. He could see the wheels turning over in her head. He wondered what plan she was making. He wanted to hear it out loud so that he could be a part of it.

When Fran pulled up to the building, Carlos hesitated in unlocking the door to let them out. The building looked worse for wear. Yet it was the best looking place on the block, and that wasn't saying much.

Carlos hopped out first. Fran went to the back door to hand Eva out. When he opened the door, she seemed surprised to see him there. Even more surprised at the offer of his hand.

"Thank you for the ride," she said.

"Name's Fran."

"I'm Eva. Thank you again, Fran. For your help back there. It was really nice to meet you, even under the circumstances."

"This isn't it." They both blinked at the vehemence in his voice. "I mean, I'd still love to have Carlos come out to the ranch for the program I was telling you about."

"We'll have to discuss it and—"

"Eva!"

They both turned to the sound of the high-pitched voice. A young girl who was the spitting image of Eva ran out of the glass doors.

"I'm so glad your home," said the girl through her trembling cries. "Someone was at the door. They knocked and knocked and wouldn't go away. They said they wanted Carlos to come out. Eva, I don't want to stay here anymore."

Eva looked around, helpless. Fran could see the crack in her countenance. His resolve was firm. It had taken the car ride for her to put herself back together, but this seemed the final straw.

"Go get your things," he said. "You're coming home with me."

CHAPTER EIGHT

*T*here were times in her life when Eva planned every detail to the last dotted I and crossed T. She'd study the situation, make notes about all the possible answers, and then come to the best conclusion.

This was the first time she'd made a split second decision.

Eva raced up the three flights of stairs to the apartment with her siblings. They pulled out bags—trash bags, because they never could afford suitcases—and packed all of their belongings in under thirty minutes. There wasn't much to pack.

Over the years, they'd grown so accustomed to being shuffled around by their relatives that they had resorted to living out of garbage and duffel bags.

They grabbed those bags now and shoved the few things they had in the small room they shared into the bellies of the bags.

A creak on the floorboards had Eva looking up. She grabbed the first weapon she could, which unfortunately happened to be a hairbrush. A gush of relief left her chest when she saw that it was Fran.

The sight of him made her feel safe and protected. She'd known the man for less than an hour. But already, he'd given her more comfort and offered to do more for her than her entire family. First, with his protection of her and her brother back at the church. Then the ride just a few miles that they could've walked or caught the bus. And now he was offering them a place to stay the night.

Eva was sure this whole thing with the street thugs would cool down. Maybe? In a couple of days? Hopefully?

God, who was she kidding? This had been brewing since they'd moved in. She knew there was no way the streets would let Carlos go unscathed. She knew her sister would continue to retreat deeper into herself beyond just staying inside four walls. And she was supposed to work her fingers to the bone to afford it all? They couldn't stay there a second longer.

"You all stayed here?" asked Fran. "In this one bedroom?"

His face was part disbelief, part disgust, shaded with a whole lot of anger.

Eva became self-conscious. Had she been selfish all these years? Should she have put all of her money into getting them a better place to live instead of trying to save for college to make her dreams come true? Maybe she was no better than her aunt?

"Take everything," said Fran. "You're not coming back here. I have plenty of room at my place."

"Just for a night or two," Eva insisted.

He didn't answer. He took her bag from her, and then Rosalee's. Eva noted that Rosalee hadn't shied away from Fran like she had most people. What was it about this guy?

Fran preceded her family down the three flights and into his truck. He loaded up the back with their things, hopped inside, and pulled away from the apartment. In the rearview mirror, Eva saw the little thugs watching their retreat.

No, they couldn't go back there. She'd figure out a new plan.

They drove for what seemed like hours, but she knew was more like thirty minutes. Buildings gave way to mountains. Concrete gave way to rolling fields. The smell of industry and fast food gave way to brisk wind and cut grass.

Peering into the back seat, she saw Carlos staring out in wonder. Rosalee had rolled down the window and was leaning her head out. Eva looked at the man beside her.

Fran's face had relaxed somewhat. His shoulders were still tense. He pumped the brakes as they pulled into a gate with a purple flower on the front. The gate opened and gave them access to a world out of a western movie.

"I've never done anything like this before," Eva confessed.

Fran turned to her, taking his eyes off the road for a moment. The second his gaze hit hers Eva felt something spark in her chest. She wondered if he felt it too? Was that the reason he jerked his gaze back to the road?

"Anything like what?" he asked.

"Hopping in a car with a strange man and spending the night with him."

"I'm not a strange man. I was invited to your church by Dr. Patel."

"Pastor Patel?"

Fran nodded. "He's a psychologist."

"Hmmm." Eva hesitated to ask her next questions.

"Yes, I am his patient."

She noted the smile in Fran's voice. But the smile slipped away with his next words.

"My entire squad is. We were all wounded in the service. Dr. Patel works on the ranch to help us."

"You have PTSD?" She tried to make her voice nonchalant and was certain she failed.

"In a manner of speaking."

"I'm so sorry if I'm offending you."

"You're not. You're a smart woman, and you're asking smart questions of the man you just ran off with to spend the night."

Eva gasped.

Fran chuckled as he made a turn.

His laugh was nice. She liked how it crinkled his face. She waited for any sign that she should run. None came. She knew she was entirely safe with this man.

"I have my demons," he said. "But they only come after me. I have never lashed out at an innocent before in my life. You're safe with me, Eva. I won't let anything happen to you or your brother and sister. You have my word."

With those words, she relaxed back into the seat of his truck.

If Eva had thought the drive up was lovely, the ranch that sprawled out before her was something out of a dream. There was green as far as the eye could see. Beyond that were mountains. What pavement there was clean and clear.

Fran parked the truck in front of a small ranch house. Eva had never lived in a house, not even when her parents were alive. They'd always lived in apartments, up off the ground floor, sharing rooms. She'd never had a yard. Across the way, a couple of dogs yipped in a neighboring yard.

The kids hopped out and greeted the dogs. No one was more surprised than Eva when Rosalee bent down to scratch at a little Chihuahua's head.

"They're all friendly," Fran assured her.

Eva hadn't thought the dogs posed a threat, especially the one in a wheelchair. She hadn't even fretted as the Rottweiler, a breed notoriously deemed vicious, trotted over to Fran. Its head was down as it made its way over followed by another dog, a Golden Retriever.

"Hey, Sugar," Fran bent over and patted the Retriever's head.

Eva had learned that dogs were the best judges

of character, and each of these dogs vied for Fran's attention alongside yipping for pats on the head from her siblings. Yes, hopping in this stranger's truck, this was a good decision.

"I'm sorry my horde of beasts got let loose. They're all harmless."

Eva looked up to see a pretty brunette closing the door of the home next to Fran's. She had a wide smile. Eva hadn't had many girlfriends because she moved around so much, and she rarely wanted to bring anyone over for sleepovers or study group or tea. She didn't even drink tea. But this woman looked like she had people over for tea.

"Maggie, this is Eva," said Fran. "She and her siblings are coming to stay with me for a while."

Maggie took Eva's hand in hers. Her palm was warm and welcoming. She covered Eva's hand with her second palm. It was like a hug for her hands.

"I'm so happy to meet you. You'll come over for dinner tonight with me and my husband. It's just hot dogs and chicken tenders—"

"Hot dogs?" said Carlos.

"Chicken tenders?" said Rosalee.

"Eva, please?" They chimed in together.

"I don't want to impose," said Eva.

"No imposition at all," said Maggie. "I'd love to get

to know you better, and I could use some help feeding the dogs if your brother and sister don't mind."

"We don't mind," said Rosalee.

Eva stared at her sister. Rosalee never invited herself over to others' houses. But there she was volunteering.

"Okay," said Eva.

CHAPTER NINE

This was a bad decision. What had he been thinking? The sight of Eva in his living room, amongst his things, had his heart going double time. This was not good for his health. Not just because the effect it was having on his heart. It was because of his heart that she couldn't stay.

He'd offered her a place to stay when this place wouldn't be his for much longer. Fran was living on borrowed time. He had no business promising any of that time to anyone, let alone someone like this family who had been abandoned and disappointed by so many in their lives.

"There are four bedrooms," said Rosalee.

Fran looked up into her bright eyes. When he'd first met the little girl, her eyes had been filled with fear. But now they sparkled with excitement, gratitude, and hope.

"Would I be allowed to sleep in one on my own?" she asked.

"Of course," Fran heard himself saying.

"Fran, that's too much," said Eva. "We don't want to put any of your roommates out."

"I don't have any roommates. It's just me. You each can stay in your own room. For as long as you like."

His tongue darted away from his teeth inside his mouth, escaping from being bitten and hushed. Maybe he could get his foot in there instead. But his feet were planted firmly on the ground as he watched Carlos and Rosalee disappear into separate bedrooms. The smiles on their faces were so big they trailed behind them.

"We won't be a bother," said Eva. "It'll just be for a couple of days. While I figure out what to do next."

"You can stay as long as you like. I want you to be safe."

He wanted to pull her back into his arms and hold her again. But she wasn't crying. She wasn't distraught. He'd made it all better just by opening his door to her.

From the corner of his eye, he saw Xavier and

Sean headed toward his front door. An idea started forming in Fran's head. Perhaps he could make this stay forever for Eva and her siblings.

"Why don't you go and get settled?" he told her.

Eva nodded. Her sigh of relief visibly shook weight from her petite frame. She took her bag from him and headed for one of the two remaining bedrooms.

"That's my bedroom," said Fran.

"Oh," she blushed. "I'm so sorry." She side-stepped and disappeared into the last bedroom. The one next to his.

Fran's heartbeat had settled, but there was still a fluttering in his chest. He felt light-headed and hungry. Instead of going to the kitchen, Fran turned to the door as Xavier and Sean came up the steps. He shut the door behind him and faced his friends.

"Heard you brought a woman home," said Xavier. He was the playboy of the bunch. X went out to the bars every weekend and spent the night with a different girl.

Fran put his back to the man and turned to Sean.

"So, you changed your mind about a wife?" asked Sean

"No, no," said Fran. "She's not for me."

Xavier and Sean looked at each other.

"You know I can't ..." Fran waved his hand in front of his heart which was still beating the same rhythm as when he'd held Eva in his arms. "But one of you could."

Sean took a step down off the porch. His eyes went wide like a steed about to be neutered. Sean hadn't lost a limb, only skin from his face that had hardened into tough scars. Because there was nothing wrong with his legs, Sean could easily outrun Fran with his heart condition.

The moment the words were out of Fran's mouth his heart did a funny little flip. It was a bit painful and he winced. "Eva and her family need a place to stay, and those kids need strong male figures in their lives."

"I told you," said Xavier. "I'm not getting married. I'll take this to court. We need to challenge this."

Sean remained quiet. He turned his scarred face away from them both.

"Eva's amazing," said Fran. "She's beautiful and smart—"

"So why don't you marry her?" said Xavier.

"I already told you—"

"Yeah-yeah, you think you're gonna die. We're all gonna die someday. If you really think marriage would help this girl and her family, you should do it.

That way, if you really die, which I doubt you'll do anytime soon, she won't have to put up with you for long."

Fran's heart stopped that flipping and settled like it liked the idea.

The door to the house opened and Carlos poked his head out. He saw Rosalee hang back in the living room. Fran wanted her to know that she was safe there. He wanted to take the girl to see the baby chickens. He wanted to teach Carlos to ride and to shoot. To show Rosalee that the world wasn't dangerous everywhere. To show Carlos what it meant to be a real man.

And he could help Eva make her plan. He could help her implement it and be there to help her correct course if something veered her off. Fran thought about the closed door of the bedroom next to his. Once again his heart did a flip.

CHAPTER TEN

*E*va ran her hand over the comforter on the bed. It looked as though it had never been slept in. The whole room looked unused but somehow cozy. She could sense Fran's presence there even though he said his room was next door. She placed her hand on the wall and was positive she felt it hum with his easy smile.

Eva jerked her hand away. What was she doing? What was she thinking?

She was staying in a stranger's house. In the bedroom right next to his. She was thinking she could feel his presence in the room, in the walls. Was she developing feelings for this guy?

She could not be developing feelings for this guy.

She had two kids to take care of. An education to get. And a living situation to figure out.

The living situation might just be figured out. Fran had said they could stay as long as they'd like, which would help both the education situation and the kid care situation.

But no. The only kindness she'd ever depended on was that of her family.

And look where that had gotten her.

They would stay here a couple of nights. Two weeks tops. That would give her time to figure things out. Or at least to get a new job. They couldn't take advantage of Fran beyond that.

Eva reached for the door to her bedroom—his bedroom. The borrowed, temporary room. She turned the knob, pulled open the door, and walked right into a wall of chest.

Fran caught her when she stumbled. His arms came around her, embracing her and holding her steady.

"I was coming to check on you," he said.

"I was coming to ..." She didn't know what she was going to say. She just didn't want to move out of his strong hold. But it was not her place. Fran let her go.

"Can we talk for a moment?" he asked.

Something in his tone made the goosebumps on her arms stand up. Had he changed his mind? Had the kids gotten into trouble?

She spied her siblings out the window in the driveway. Carlos played basketball with two men. Rosalee sat watching the game as she petted two dogs.

Eva trailed Fran into the living room. His movements were jerky. His hand rubbed at the back of his neck, lifting the short tendrils of hair at his nape until they stood up. He took the seat opposite from her. He was nervous. She could tell.

"Eva, there's a slight problem with you staying here."

She knew it. She knew it was all too good to be true. Nausea sent basketballs around in her belly that constantly missed the hoop.

"It was impulsive of me to ask you to stay."

"It's okay. We can go."

"No," he said, raising his hands up in a stop motion. "That's not what I'm saying. I want you here."

Relief flooded her. The balls in her belly stopped bouncing. But they didn't hold still. Something told her the game wasn't over.

"I want you all here. There's just a condition that I should've told you about before bringing you here."

"What condition?"

He wouldn't meet her gaze. He also stumbled over his words. She'd only known him a couple of hours, but she knew instinctively that this was uncharacteristic behavior for him.

"The ranch was purchased as a rehabilitation facility for wounded veterans."

"I see. And I'm not a vet."

"That's not it. You don't have to be a vet to stay here. You have to be ..."

He took a deep breath. He lifted his head and met her gaze. But his words stalled as he bit at his lip and scratched at the fabric covering his chest.

"We've been here for a year, but the paperwork was slow to go through. We found a hiccup with the zoning."

Eva nodded encouragingly as he hesitated to get to the point.

"The zoning is for families only. You have to be a family to live here."

"I have a family," she said, certain she was missing something.

"Technically, you're single. And so am I. So are

most of the guys living here, except Dylan. He and Maggie just got married."

"So, I'd have to be a married woman to live here?"

Fran nodded. "So do I. Be a married man, I mean. Otherwise, I'll have to leave soon."

"So, you're getting married?"

"Getting married would solve the problem. It would solve both our problems."

"Marriage?"

Fran nodded.

She was still missing something ... Wait? "You're asking *me* to marry *you*."

"It would solve the problem," he repeated.

Eva checked her pulse. It wasn't racing. Just like it hadn't raced when she'd hopped in the truck with Fran and let him drive her away. He'd just asked her to marry him, and she was calm. A life with Fran didn't scare her in the least.

"So you want to get married now and get divorced later?" The thought of marriage hadn't kicked up her heartbeat. It sounded like the most natural thing in the world. The thought of divorcing Fran, however, made her stomach burn and left a bitter taste in her mouth.

"No, no need to get divorced."

So, he wanted to be with her forever? Now her heart did flip and flop. She had never been one for fairy tales or knights and castles. But Fran had just whisked her off in storybook fashion. Now he was throwing in a happily-ever-after.

"I won't be here long," he said.

"You're leaving?"

He hesitated. "Yes, in a manner of speaking. I'm dying."

He held his tongue, waiting for her to digest that pronouncement. She had to have heard him wrong. He couldn't have said what she thought he'd said.

"Dying?"

Fran slipped a button of his shirt open. Eva's emotions were already all over the place with his kindness in providing her family a safe haven, then with his proposal of marriage, and now he was showing her the goods so to speak. But the goods were a series of scars on his chest where his heart would rest.

"I have shrapnel in my chest," he said. "It's inoperable. The metal fragments could shift at any moment in the wrong direction and kill me."

Eva stared at him, at those eyes that hid nothing from her and made her feel safe. He was telling her that someday soon she wouldn't be able to look into those eyes. She'd rested her head on his chest. But someday soon she wouldn't be able to come into his arms and feel safe, because he'd be gone.

"The zoning of this land requires that only families live on the ranch. I have until next month, and then I'll need to leave. If we married, I could spend the rest of my days here with my squad, and you and your family could live here indefinitely."

Eva ran his words through her head again and then again.

"You could go to school and not worry about finding a place to stay. Your brother and sister would be safe and surrounded by people who would look out for them, especially Carlos. He'd have half a dozen male role models that would lead him down the straight path. Rosalee would feel safe coming outside. And you, you could finally have your dream of going to college and finishing that plan you started."

It was a dream. She was in a dream. This all had to be some cruel, wonderful, sick, delightful, twisted dream.

"But what about you?" she asked. "What if you live long, you'd be stuck with us."

Fran shrugged. "It's been a good day, so far."

But Eva didn't laugh, she couldn't.

"I could make it another year, maybe two. If I go on living any longer, I wouldn't contest a divorce ... if you wanted one."

"I wouldn't ... I mean, I wouldn't abandon you."

"So, is that a yes?"

CHAPTER ELEVEN

*F*ran stood at the railing as he watched Sean help Rosalee mount Bailey, a gentle mare. He hadn't missed Rosalee's smile or the fact that Sean gave her his scarred side. Stevie, the nearly blind Rottweiler sat quietly in the field. None of Maggie's dogs had any fear of the horses.

Star, the Pug with patches missing from her skin, trotted close to Carlos's heel as Carlos and Xavier led another horse out to pasture.

The kids had fallen in with ranch life like they'd been born to it. They'd spent all day Saturday running about like wild creatures amongst the farm animals. They hadn't hesitated to lend a hand with any chore asked of them. At dinner last night, they'd attacked Maggie's grade-school fare of chicken nuggets and hot dogs with a gusto and then surprised all the adults by offering to do the dishes and take out the dogs.

Eva had been mostly quiet through the whole affair. Fran had caught her sneaking glances at him every now and again. The moment his gaze met hers, she'd turn away.

She still hadn't given him an answer to his proposal. He told himself to be patient, it had been less than forty-eight hours that he'd asked. About the same amount of time since he'd met her.

She'd asked for time to think about it. And he'd given her her space. But he was aching for a bit of claustrophobia. She'd hung back with Maggie today. He itched to know what the two were talking about.

Fran knew the plan of marriage was the best plan for all involved. He would not let them go back to that neighborhood or that dismal apartment. He'd heard their family motto of no charity.

This wasn't charity. It was common sense. He just hoped she would put aside her pride and see it too.

"What's crawled up your butt?" said Reed.

"I asked Eva to marry me yesterday."

Reed hadn't seemed surprised, likely because he already knew. Fran had told Dylan, and he was sure

Dylan had told Maggie, or Eva had told Maggie. But that was all it took on the ranch. Once one person knew your business, everyone knew it. So there was no sense in hiding it.

"She'll say yes," said Reed. "You think she'd pass up on all this." Reed spread his arms, his fleshy one as well as his prosthetic one, around the ranch.

"She's not some gold digger."

"This place isn't filled with gold, DeMonti. It was a joke."

But Fran was too grumpy for humor. He just wanted to know she'd be safe.

Reed stared at him. "You like this girl, don't you? Otherwise, I'd be able to make a comment about her without you jumping down my throat."

"I just ... want to help."

Reed nodded. "Like you said the other day, she's a smart girl. She loves her family and will do what's best for them. So clearly, she'll pass you over and choose me. Kidding."

Reed held up his hand when Fran glared at him. Fran's heart pounded in his chest at the thought of Eva and Reed, or Eva and anyone else. Which was selfish of him. He wouldn't be around forever, and she'd need to move on after he was gone. Still, the thought made his shoulders cave in. Fran gripped his chest at the shock of pain.

"You good?" asked Reed coming over to him.

"Yeah," Fran said taking a deep breath. "It's over now."

Every once in a while, the shrapnel in his chest reminded him of its presence. Luckily, this time it was a reminder and not a last call. Fran wanted to make it official between him and Eva before his curtain came down. That way she'd be protected for the rest of her life.

"Uncle Fran, look! I'm riding."

Fran looked up at Rosalee on the horse. He plastered a smile on his face and waved at the girl. Both she and her brother had taken to calling all of the soldiers *uncle*. The sight of little Rosalee smiling made his heart ache a bit more. He wanted to teach her so many things, watch her grow in confidence. Even if Eva said no, he'd figure out a way to keep them all safe.

"Hey, Uncle Reed." Carlos came up to them. He extended his hand and gave Reed a complicated handshake that the two of them made up at some point yesterday.

Neither of the kids balked at the injuries each of the soldiers faced. They didn't know what Fran's injury was, just that he had one. But they hadn't asked, and Fran wasn't inclined to tell them. He didn't want to scare them.

"Uncle Fran, can I go with Uncle Xavier down to the pond? He said I needed to ask your permission."

Fran hesitated. He should consult Eva about this. Yeah, ... he should consult Eva about this. He should go and find her and make sure it was fine with her.

"You go on," said Fran. "I'll let your sister know where you are. But mind everything Xavier tells you. Do I have your word?"

"You have my word." Carlos loved giving his word. His chest puffed out every time one of the soldiers asked him for it. Then the kid strove to do all he could to keep that word.

Fran knew he'd grow into a fine young man. He'd give the kid all the time he could to help him on that trajectory. But for now, he'd go and talk with his sister about their immediate future.

CHAPTER TWELVE

"You married him within a week of knowing him?"

Maggie nodded. Her eyes getting that glazed faraway look of someone deeply in love. The two women sat at Eva's kitchen table.

Well, no. It was Fran's kitchen table. Though serving Maggie a glass of lemonade made Eva feel like the mistress of the house.

She'd found things easily in the cupboards. She'd likely have to attribute that to Fran. His organization system made sense. Cups over the sink. Plates over the stove. Silverware in the drawer next to the stove.

When Maggie had asked to come over after dinner the other night, Eva had cut up fresh lemons and put them in filtered water with some sugar.

She'd rarely had fresh lemonade. The fresh lemons themselves were usually more expensive than the cheap bottled, store-brand gallons. Fran even had some mint that she tossed in the mixture.

He'd given her free reign of the kitchen and the fridge. That morning before he and the kids left, she'd made a huge breakfast. Pancakes, eggs, sausage, and a fresh fruit salad. She hadn't eaten like that since her parents had still been with them.

She'd worried it had been too much. The look on Fran's face when he'd seen the fare told her it was perfect. He vocalized his appreciation around mouthfuls of food as he chatted with her siblings about their plans for the day. Eva had begged off, telling them she had some thinking to do.

Fran had given her a meaningful look when she'd said that. She still hadn't given him an answer to his marriage proposal. She wasn't sure what held her back? Nothing did. She only knew that something should.

"So, it was love at first sight?" she asked Maggie.

"It was something at first sight. I don't know if I'd call it love, but love came quickly. The first time I saw Dylan, I knew he was someone I could trust, someone who'd keep me and my dogs safe."

Eva had felt the same way about Fran. She'd felt

safe in his arms. She'd known he would keep her and her siblings safe. The thought of a lifetime of safety sounded good to her.

"You know, he's ... not in the best of health?" said Maggie.

There was that. "Is it as dire as he says? There's no hope?"

Maggie shrugged. "After the month I've had, I believe in miracles. What I do know for sure is that Fran is one of the best of them. All these guys are. I saw the way he looks at you."

That piqued Eva's attention. Fran had been looking at her? She'd felt something between them, but she had such little experience with men she wasn't sure if she was reading it right.

"I haven't known him long, but I saw that same look in Dylan's eyes when he proposed to me."

"You don't think it's crazy that I'm even considering this? Well, of course, you don't. You married quickly. The funny thing is we met at the church while I was giving a talk about preparing for the future."

"Let me guess," said Maggie. "Pastor Patel asked you to speak?"

"Yes, he did. Do you know him?"

"I know him, all right." Maggie grinned, her gaze

softening once more. But it was how Eva used to look at her father.

"Right, Fran said he works here with the soldiers."

"Hmmm." Maggie's eyes reflected the light of mischief. "You could call it that."

"I want to get married. I want my education too. But getting married for a place to live, I don't know?"

"It's more than a place to live. It's a family. This land belongs to Dylan now. It'll take him some time to get the zoning changed so anyone can live here. In the meantime, no matter what, or when, you'd have a place here. You and your family would have people who have your back here, whether you wanted us to or not."

The tone of Maggie's voice sounded as if she was trying to sound threatening but failed. Her words sounded like heaven to Eva. A knock sounded at the back door. When they turned, Fran poked his head in.

"You don't have to knock on your own door," said Eva.

"I didn't want to interrupt," he said coming inside. His gaze fastened on her, and she felt her cheeks heat.

"I was just about to head out," said Maggie. She

gave Eva a squeeze. "See you at dinner in the hall tonight, okay?"

Eva let go of Maggie's friendly embrace and turned to Fran. They were alone. Though he stood apart from her, she felt the heat from him. Just being close to him made her body settle like feet sinking into the sand, or better yet, a seed settling into rich soil.

"I'm not here to pressure you about that question I asked you the other day," he said.

Was that disappointment she felt sinking in her chest?

"You can take your time on that," he said.

"I thought we didn't have much time."

"We'll make time. It's a big decision, and I want you to be sure. I just came to tell you that Carlos ..."

Whatever Fran said afterward trailed off like the volume slowly being turned down on a television set. Eva watched his lips move. The hum of his deep voice felt good as it traveled through her eardrums and into her head. For someone so level-headed, Fran made her feel dizzy.

She snapped back to attention when silence filled the room. He was waiting for her response. Patient as always. Like a tree that had been there for centuries, strong and solid.

"Yes," she said.

"So, it's okay that Carlos goes fishing at the pond?"

"What?"

"Carlos. I told him it was okay, but I wanted to double check with you. If it's not okay, I'll go get him."

"It's fine. I trust you and all of the guys here. That's not what I was saying yes to."

She heard his breath catch. Fran's gaze locked on her. She felt like a target, and he was a heat-seeking missile.

He took a step toward her. "What were you saying yes to?"

Eva swallowed. She was certain, but that hadn't stopped her hands from shaking and her heart from going a mile a minute.

"Yes," she repeated. "Yes, I'll marry you."

They stood, gazing at each other from across the room. Eva wanted to run to him, to envelope herself in his arms and stay. But she held still, unsure of exactly what to do.

"I'll take care of everything," he said.

Eva was pretty sure that those were the sexiest words a man could ever say to a woman. "I trust you."

His grin spread as though those were the sexiest words a woman could ever say to a man.

"Of course, our marriage will be platonic."

Eva blinked. She cocked her head to the side to shake the words into a comprehensible order. No matter the arrangement, the meaning came out the same.

"I wouldn't ask that of you."

"Right," she said in a halfhearted, tepid tone. "Of course not."

The thought of sex hadn't entered her mind. But she doubted it was far from her mind. Hearing that it was off the table? Well, it hadn't exactly thrilled her.

She supposed it made sense. They'd just met. And he was dying. And this was a marriage of convenience. They weren't in love.

Still, her heart thumped an erratic rhythm at what she would not be offered on the plate.

CHAPTER THIRTEEN

"Was it love at first sight?" asked Rosalee.

Fran looked down at his bride's little sister. Rosalee stood at the gazebo with Fran in the late afternoon sun. She was dressed in a new dress that he'd bought for her.

Fran had seen the girl eyeing the dress that morning as they went to grab a few essentials for the ceremony. Eva had turned over the price tag and pinched her lips together. Fran hadn't even looked at the tag, but grabbed the dress from the rack and put it in the cart.

Before Eva could protest, he'd said the words that had shut her mouth when he'd purchased their rings and a small bouquet of flowers. "We're family now."

And just like that, the words stopped her protest. He realized he could get away with a lot with those three words. But they didn't suffice in answer to the kids' questions.

"Are you gonna be, like, my dad now?" asked Carlos. He hadn't asked for any new clothes, but Fran had still purchased him a white collared shirt to wear with his jeans. The kid fidgeted in the stiff clothes.

"Well, she's your sister," said Fran, choosing to answer the easier of the two questions launched at him. "So, that would make us brothers."

Carlos grinned at that idea. His head bobbed in a nod as his shoulders straightened.

"When did you realize you loved Eva?" Rosalee pressed.

"Obviously, in the last couple of days, Rosie," Carlos said. "Otherwise why would he be marrying her. That's why people get married, right? Because they're in love."

"Or because the girl got pregnant," said Rosalee.

Carlos turned shocked, mutinous eyes on Fran. Pride filled Fran's chest as he watched the young boy's hackles rise to think anyone would take advantage of his older sister.

"Eva's not pregnant," Fran assured him. Turning

to Rosalee, he tried an academic argument. "Marriage isn't just about love. It's about protection, property, financial stability. It establishes rights and obligations that the government will recognize."

Both kids frowned at him as though they were sitting in the back of the class, and he was droning on at the lectern.

"I liked your sister from the first moment I saw her. Just like I liked you all when we first met. I wanted to be a part of your family, and I wanted you to be my family."

"You could've adopted us," said Rosalee. She was a smart kid.

"True," Fran said.

"You don't have to marry Eva for that."

"I want to marry Eva." That came out a bit more vehemently than Fran had planned.

She didn't say it, but he saw the question why in the sparkle of Rosalee's eyes. Eyes so like her sister's. Thankfully, he didn't have to answer that question as he saw movement in the distance.

Two golf carts pulled up. The first contained Reed, Sean, Xavier, and Dr. Patel who would be officiating the ceremony. In the second golf cart was Dylan, Maggie, and Eva.

Fran's eyes caught and held on the second golf

SHANAE JOHNSON

cart. He couldn't see what Eva was wearing. She was sitting in the back seat. But he could see her face.

Her face was tilted up to the sun, as though drinking it in. Her nostrils flared, and her shoulders lifted as she took a deep breath. Was she nervous? Was she having second thoughts?

Fran felt his heart give a kick. He wanted to run to her, to grab hold of her and do what it took to convince her that this was the right decision. The thought of her going back to that apartment. The thought of not seeing her inside his home, having her close to protect. The thought of her not frowning up at him as he threw down his credit card to buy her and her siblings whatever their hearts demanded. Well, he did not like any of those thoughts.

As though she'd heard him, Eva's face tilted down. Her eyes opened, and her gaze found his.

A twinge went through Fran's heart. A twisting ache that rattled his teeth. He battled through the pain, not allowing it to show on his face. Even if the shrapnel chose that moment to take his life, he would make sure Eva saw him smiling at her.

Thankfully, the twinge died down by the time everyone was in place, and Eva walked toward him at the gazebo. He was sure there was music, as he

94

saw Reed with speakers. He was sure words were
said to him, as he was vaguely aware of Dr. Patel's
lips moving. But Fran's eyes held rapt to Eva.

She wore a simple dress; one she insisted on
buying with her own money. It was little more than a
white sundress, made of cotton with a lace trim. It
sat on her strong shoulders, the lace making those
shoulders look delicate. The dress grabbed at her
bodice making Fran's palms itch to do the same. And
then it flowed down around her torso, touching the
tops of her knees. Strappy sandals completed the
look.

She was a vision. He knew that when the metal
finally took him and his life was flashing before his
eyes, that vision would hold for long moments
before he turned into the light.

"You look beautiful." It was the first words he'd
said to her. He realized those words weren't said at
the proper time as Dr. Patel cleared his throat with a
smile, and the audience gathered sent up a chuckle.

Fran shut his mouth, but he hadn't apologized
for telling the truth. Eva did look beautiful. He
wanted to hand over his credit card to her to buy
more dresses just like that one so that he could gaze
at her loveliness every day, instead of seeing her in
ill-fitting jeans and T-shirts. He wanted to look down

and see her painted toenails instead of scuffed sneakers and well-worn, black flats.

He would do that, he silently promised her. He knew if he said it out loud, well, he'd interrupt the ceremony again. But he also knew that she would refuse. Anything he gave her would have to be done in stealth mode. At least until she realized that everything he had was all her due.

"Francisco?"

Fran pulled his attention away from Eva and turned to Dr. Patel. The doctor seemed to have been waiting for him to respond for a moment by the way his patient eyes looked at him. "Yes?"

"It's time for the vows. Will you repeat after me?"

"Yes, of course."

"I, Francisco DeMonti, take you, Eva Barry, to be no other than yourself."

Fran repeated the words. With each statement, he realized the truth of the statements.

"Loving what I know of you, trusting what I do not yet know, I will respect your integrity and have faith in your abiding love for me, through all our years, and in all that life may bring us."

Fran had first been taken by Eva's integrity and moral character. She strove to be the best she could be and to hold her head high in a world that was constantly pushing and shoving at her. There might not be love between them, but he would take the best care of this woman she'd ever known. He'd treat her with kindness and tenderness every day that he drew breath. He would provide for her and protect her and everyone she held dear.

"Eva, I take you as my wife, with your faults and your strengths, as I offer myself to you with my faults and strengths. I will help you when you need help and turn to you when I need help. I choose you as the person with whom I will spend my life."

Tears glistened in Eva's eyes at this final pronouncement. Fran's heart pounded in his chest, but there was no pain this time. Just the beating of truth. Though this marriage was one of convenience, she must have known he meant every word he'd said.

As she repeated the same words to him, he felt his own eyes burn with the light of her truth. Just as she'd spoken fiercely about her family and her dreams, she spoke her promise to him. Her tone resonating with sincerity and veracity. Though he'd stopped speaking, Fran's throat was raw as he took her words in.

He knew, without a doubt, that she meant each of them. He believed her when she said she took

SHANAE JOHNSON

him with his faults. He knew she'd be a help at every turn. He was honored that she chose him, that he would spend the rest of his life, however long, with her.

"You may now kiss your bride."

Fran's lips parted before Dr. Patel finished speaking. The ache that had been in his heart migrated to his fingertips. His breath quickened causing his lips to dry out. He snaked his tongue out to moisten them.

How had he forgotten that part? His and Eva's was to be a platonic marriage, save this one kiss. But it was tradition, expected. He had to get on with it.

He moved in slowly, carefully. He placed one palm on her shoulder, to keep her steady or to hold himself steady, he wasn't sure. He placed the other hand at her cheek to tilt her head up to his.

He swallowed down his desire, telling it that it had no place in that moment. That it was just the culmination of a ritual, an end to the ceremony. But Fran couldn't get past the lump in his throat.

Eva let out a small sigh as he came closer. Her breath was the sweetest thing he'd ever tasted in his life. It soothed the dryness of his lips. So, he came closer.

He pressed his lower lip to her upper lip. The

98

first brush of her soft lips felt like the strongest wind. He would not let it knock him down. He pressed forward. He'd only meant for the kiss to be a brief connection of lips. He was a fool to think he could stop there.

His thumb came under her chin, tilting her head back a bit more, to give him better access. When he felt no resistance, he captured both her lips in his, and knew he was lost.

CHAPTER FOURTEEN

*E*va had been kissed before. She'd had a couple of dates in high school. There'd been a handful of guys who'd piqued her interest in the years after.

Kissing the high school boys had been mostly a bumping of noses, gnashing of teeth, and a sloppy exchange of spit. The men afterward, had been only a bit better, with a nice warmth from the press of lips, and a few interesting licks of the tongue.

What was happening in her mouth with Fran, in a crowd of onlookers, was nothing like what she'd experienced in all of her dating life.

There was no bumping or gnashing as Fran's hand expertly tilted her head exactly where he wanted her to go. So dazed by his nearness, she'd given him complete control of her head, of her body, of herself.

Fran's lips were warm against hers. But the heat went beyond nice. He pressed into her mouth using only the firm softness of his lips. If he'd introduced his tongue, Eva was certain she'd have expired on the spot.

He captured both of her lips with his. But he'd taken hold of more than her lips. Her heart thumped an increasing beat, as though it were marching toward him. Her brain fogged and then cleared, like a cloud moving out of the sun's way.

Everything was so clear. She saw her entire life laid out for her, a life with this man, folded into the safety of his arms.

For so long she'd thought school had been her dream. She saw it clearly now. School was a goal. Fran had been her dream. A dream she hadn't known she'd had until that very moment.

The tip of his tongue darted out and tasted the fleshy part at the center of her upper lip. And just like in the storybooks, like in the teen angst movies, like in the soapy, romantic dramas on the small screen, Eva let out a swooning sigh.

Luckily, she hadn't fainted. She'd stayed on her feet. She'd had too. She wasn't about to miss a second of that kiss. And, man oh man, it did not disappoint.

Fran pulled away, leaving her bereft. But he did not let her go. He encased her in his arms, holding her close. His breath was heavy against her ear, his voice shaky as he spoke.

"I've got you," he said.

He did have her. All of her. Eva laid her head against his heart. It beat a rapid rhythm. She wondered if that was bad. It couldn't be. It had to mean he was feeling what she was feeling. She would keep his heart beating for as long as she could.

"I now pronounce you, husband and wife."

Eva opened her eyes to see Pastor Patel smiling at her, at them both. He had that sparkle in his eye, the same sparkle he'd had when he'd asked her to speak at the church event.

Had he known? Had he known that she and Fran would wind up in this very spot?

Pastor Patel hadn't balked when they'd asked him to perform their ceremony after only knowing each other for less than three days. In fact, he'd had that weekend free which was unusual for such a busy man of the church and a doctor with a booming practice.

Applause sounded from around the gazebo. Eva stepped back from Fran's embrace, remembering that they weren't alone. All of Fran's friends filled the area. The only people to represent Eva were her brother and sister.

She'd called her aunt and a few other family members. But they all said they couldn't make it so far on such short notice. The drive was only thirty minutes, and she doubted they had much else to do.

But whatever.

She was very happy at the turn out of people who cared about her. Rosalee sat next to Maggie. Both girls grinning and whispering to each other while clapping their hands. Carlos sat between Reed and Sean. Her little brother looked all grown up in his new shirt and his hair combed back.

"I present to you, Mr. and Mrs. Fran and Eva DeMonti."

Eva's heart gave another lurch at the sound of her new name. The lurch wasn't of fear. It was the feeling of settling in, clicking into place.

Fran took her hand, wrapping his fingers around hers as they made their way down the steps of the gazebo.

The lunch reception was a blur of stories of Fran. Questions fired at her to get to know her better.

Being twirled around by each of Fran's fellow soldiers. And then she was in Fran's arms again, swaying slowly to a sappy Top 40's song.

"No regrets?" he asked as he gazed down at her.

"Not a single one." She bit her lip at the forwardness of her response. She had to remember that this was still a marriage of convenience, not one of love. Not yet anyway. "What about you?"

"I meant those vows, Eva. I plan to take very good care of you and your family so long as I'm here."

That threw cold water on her warm emotions. Fran constantly reminded her of his failing heart. But all she could focus on was how generously it beat for all those around him.

She'd watch him give of himself to his brothers. And now he gave all he could to her and her siblings. She'd let him take care of them. That didn't mean she couldn't take care of him too.

"About that kiss," he began.

Eva felt her cheeks heating. Not from embarrassment. She hoped he was about to bless her with another kiss.

"I'm sorry about that," he said.

"You're ... sorry?"

"I guess I just got caught up in ... everything. It won't happen again."

"It ... won't?"

"You have to know I don't expect any of ... that from you."

"Right. No affection."

"That's not what I meant." Fran seemed to struggle. "I care about you. I care a lot. I don't mean I'll be cold to you. Or that I won't offer you my arm or my hand when we're out walking. Or that I won't hug you when I see you or hold you when you need a strong arm."

"That's good. I like hugs."

Fran pulled her closer as they continued to sway to the song. "You can have all the hugs you want."

But no more kisses? Still, being inside of Fran's arms was the best feeling in the world. She'd content herself with that.

For now.

CHAPTER FIFTEEN

"*A*re we gonna change our last names? Or will you?"

Fran glanced in the rearview mirror at Rosalee. The kid was filled with questions since the ceremony yesterday.

She was strapped into the back seat of his truck in another new shirt and matching skirt set. She hugged her backpack to her small chest. Brown, inquisitive eyes stared back at him in the glass reflection.

"Only Eva changes her name," Carlos answered his sister.

"When my friend Lisa got a new dad she changed her name, too. It was hyphenated."

Carlos considered that.

"Her stepdad adopted her," Rosalee continued to press.

"Rosie, Fran isn't adopting you," said Eva.

"That's something we can discuss," said Fran.

Eva's mouth gaped at the pronouncement. Her pupils flicked rapidly, left to right like she was trying to read between the lines. Like always, there was nothing hidden in his words. Fran said what he meant.

"I'd like to hyphenate," said Rosalee. "So we have a piece of mom and dad and a piece of Fran."

Eva turned back and faced forward. From her profile, Fran saw her throat work. She was holding back emotion.

"Yeah," said Carlos. "That sounds good to me. After the adoption, I'll hyphenate too."

"What will you do when you have kids of your own?" asked Rosalee. "I guess they'll be DeMonti."

Now Fran faced entirely forward, eyes on the road, hands gripping the steering wheel. They hadn't addressed much of the truth of their marriage with the kids. Rosalee and Carlos hadn't even realized that Fran and Eva hadn't slept in the same bedroom last night.

They'd waited until after the kids had gone to bed to slip inside their respective rooms. It hadn't been just a slip inside. Fran had walked Eva to her room. He'd tried not to stare at her. She was still dressed in the sundress from the ceremony but her feet were bare on the hardwood floors. He'd found himself staring at her pink toes.

When he'd lifted his gaze, he was met with the curves he'd been trying to ignore all day. A little higher and there was her beautiful face, still flushed from the day's excitement. They'd laughed until they were hoarse, danced until they were sore, and ate until they were glutted. It was the best day Fran had had all year, in many years.

As they stood at her bedroom door, Eva's hair was loosened from the do she'd worn earlier. Her hair was a halo around her face, making her look like a sleepy angel. Fran itched to push a strand back behind her ear.

He clenched his fist instead. Like he'd done when instinct drove his fingers to hold her hand while they sat side by side at the picnic table. Like he'd done when impulse put his lips next to her ear to whisper something funny while they danced. He'd pulled his hand away before taking hers in his. He'd turned his head to the side before confiding in her.

He had to constantly remind himself that this wasn't a real marriage, it wasn't a love relationship. It was a convenience, a means to an end to keep her and her family safe, and to allow him to spend the rest of his days near those who cared about him.

But that night, after his friends had left them to their home and after the kids had gone to sleep, as he stood with his new wife outside her bedroom door, Eva had slipped inside his arms. He'd told her she could. It was the only thing she'd asked of him.

Hugs.

Fran's arms came around her. His palms met her warm flesh. His nose came to rest atop that cloud of hair. And it was heaven.

She hadn't said anything. Just rested her head against his heart for a moment. Then she'd let him go and slipped inside her bedroom door. Fran had stood outside her door for long moments after, waiting for his heartbeat to settle and his desire to cool.

This was a convenience. It wasn't real. It couldn't be real, because it wouldn't last. There would be no tall children with long limbs and brown eyes. But there were these two children in his care, and he would do everything to make sure that Carlos and Rosalee were cared for.

"I'm so sorry we're taking you out of your way," Eva said as Fran pulled up to the kids' school.

The middle school was a twenty-minute drive from the ranch. There was no school bus service that far. Someone from the ranch would have to drive them every day.

"I'll figure out the city bus service soon—"

"Absolutely not," said Fran. "They're not taking a twenty-minute bus ride every day. And neither are you."

Eva did a double take. Fran shrugged. He would not budge on this.

"If I'm busy then one of the guys will take them," he said. "Or you can just take the truck and take them yourself."

"I can't take your truck from you."

"Then let me buy you your own car."

"I can't let you buy me a car."

"Why not?"

"Because it would take me forever to pay you back."

"I'm your husband," Fran said patiently. "What's mine is yours. And your siblings'."

"You can buy me a car," said Carlos.

"You can earn a car by doing work around the ranch," said Fran.

"Deal," Carlos agreed.

Fran looked to Rosalee. He knew that smart little girl was paying attention. He was right.

"I want a bike," she said.

"That's doable. Your sister and I will discuss how you can earn it."

Eva sat silently next to him. She didn't look upset. Just a bit shell-shocked.

Fran pulled up to the school drop-off point. He reached back and gave Carlos some dap. Rosalee leaned across her seat and gave her sister a hug. Then she turned to Fran and gave him a kiss on the cheek. Once the kids were inside the doors, Fran pulled back into traffic.

"Did I overstep my bounds back there?" he asked after a couple of miles of silence.

"No," Eva said quietly. "You just made our boundaries bigger."

"That's a good thing, right?"

"Yes." She turned to him. Her smile was more in her eyes than on her lips. "I'm not used to this, Fran. I'm not used to having a partner. I'm not used to having help with all of my responsibilities. I'm not used to giving them anything beyond the basics. They deserve more."

"You do, too."

"You're not buying me a car," she said firmly.

Fran didn't bother hiding his grin. "Not for a while."

She shook her head at him, but her smile had spread. Not just across her face. Her smile had spread to him. It crawled over his skin and then seeped inside, like rays of sunlight.

He pulled up to her campus. There was a drop-off spot called Kiss and Ride. The sign stared them in the face.

Eva released the seatbelt. She placed her hand on the door handle. Before opening the door, she turned to him. Releasing the handle, she put her hand on his chest. She leaned over, coming closer to him.

Her lips met the side of his face, but she might as well have kissed him on the lips. Her soft lips hit him hard in the gut. It took everything not to turn to her and take her mouth, staking his claim, his rightful claim, to this woman, his wife. But he held still.

"Thank you, Fran."

"Have a good day at school," he said. "I'll be right here when you finish."

She smiled at him again, mostly with her eyes. She removed her hand from his heart. It pounded in protest. Fran watched her until she disappeared inside.

CHAPTER SIXTEEN

*E*va remembered each of her first days of school. The first day of kindergarten she'd come with a new outfit, her lunchbox, and shared her cookies with Mary Bennett. Her first day of middle school, she'd gotten a new backpack and had put her Trapper Keeper inside with colorful dividers for each of her classes. The first day of high school, she'd been in hand-me-downs and last year's binder that sported duct tape to hold it together. Lunch had been courtesy of the Free Lunch program. That was the first year both her parents had died.

She wore a comfortable pair of jeans and a new top today. It was a top she'd gotten when she'd purchased her wedding dress. She'd had a bit left over since she hadn't had to buy food for the week. She hadn't had to spend a dime on anyone but herself that weekend.

Fran had taken care of everything. From her living situation, to her siblings' care, to putting food on the table. Food, clothes, and shelter. And now he wanted to buy her a car. All of this and she wasn't even putting out!

She laughed to herself as she walked into the university's School of Science building. She wanted to put out for her husband. She wanted to know what it would be like to get lost inside Fran's arms, beneath his solid frame, maybe even on top of his big body.

Eva's cheeks heated. She'd never had such bold thoughts before. She'd never met someone who'd inspired them before. With just a few, likely chaste by most standards, kisses, and she was a wanton woman.

But she wasn't a wanton woman. She was a wife. She was a wife who wanted her husband.

Her phone buzzed. Reaching into her pocket, she pulled it out to see that it was a text message from Maggie wishing her luck on her first day.

Eva noted there was also a message in her email.

It was a picture of Reed, Sean, and Xavier wearing glasses and holding books. In the first picture, they tried to look serious and failed hilariously. In the second picture, they made funny faces. The text below the pictures wished her a good first day.

She hadn't remembered giving any of them her phone number or email. But she supposed with men who were in the army, and one of them who specialized in technology, that it wasn't that hard to get her information. She was touched that they'd gone through the trouble.

They were more than just her new family; they were also her new friends. And that's what friends did for each other.

"Are you lost?"

Eva looked up to find a guy leaning against a doorway watching her. He looked like what could stereotypically be called a preppy kid with his collared shirt and pleated pants and parted hair.

"You had this faraway look in your eyes," he said, pushing off from the doorway. "I figure you're either lost or high?"

"I'm not high."

He raised his eyebrow.

"I don't do drugs."

"Me neither."

Eva didn't buy it. There was a spark in his eyes. But it was mischievous, not inquisitive.

"What room are you looking for?" He snatched the schedule out of her hand. "Oh, Professor Newton. He's a snoozer. But I know a guy who can get you his tests so you can ace the class."

"No, thank you." Eva snatched her schedule back.

"Why don't I walk you to class." It wasn't a question. He simply fell into step beside her.

"I'm good, actually."

"Just thought you might like a friend seeing that you're new."

Eva stopped in her tracks. She turned to face this guy. "I'm not lost. I'm exactly where I'm supposed to be. I don't buy tests; I do the work. And I have all the friends I need, thank you."

She scratched at her nose, even though it didn't itch. She let the ring finger of her left hand rub up and down her cheek a few times until the guy got the hint.

"You're married." The guy frowned.

"Yes," Eva confirmed. "Happily. And I'm about to be late to class. So, if you'll excuse me ..."

She turned and marched down the hall toward

her class. She found a seat near the front. There were quite a few seats open.

Professor Newton walked in with a folio of papers. Eva took out her pen as the lecture began. Five minutes after the lecture began, more students rolled in and took up seats, all in the back.

The professor wasn't boring. His voice was a bit monotone, but the picture he painted with his knowledge was fascinating. Eva's pen hadn't stopped moving for the whole class period. She noted that she was one of the only students using pen and paper, if they were taking notes at all. Most had laptops and were typing away as the professor spoke.

"Excuse me?"

Eva looked over to see a young woman next to her.

"Did you happen to catch what he said about coefficients? I got a bit lost."

"Oh, yeah, sure." Eva shuffled through her papers. She found what she was looking for and handed the document to the woman.

"Oh, no, no. Would you mind just repeating it back to me? I have a whole system of note taking, and I need to put it in its proper place. I know that sounds weird."

"No, it makes sense to me. My next class doesn't

start for thirty minutes. You wanna grab something to drink and we can compare notes? Maybe a cup of tea?"

"I'd like that. I'm Jan Collison."

"Eva Lopez ... DeMonti. Lopez-DeMonti."

CHAPTER SEVENTEEN

"Steady there," Fran coaxed both animal and boy.

Carlos looked like a grown man from his perch on the horse. Fran was certain the boy felt grown up from his high seat there. There was something about being in the seat of a horse that changed a man's perspective.

Fran led the young man and his steed on a path through the ranch. So much had changed in a week. Fran spied Rosalee working in the garden alongside Sean and the dogs. Maggie and Dylan were necking on the side of the barn, believing no one could see them.

Carlos had taken to ranch life like he'd been

born to it. The kid was up at dawn, doing chores before school. After he finished his homework, he was back out helping the other men with errands before sundown.

Rosalee was often out of the house and by her brother's side. All the signs of agoraphobia and social anxieties had all but disappeared.

That's what the ranch was all about. It healed everyone who came within the gates be they vet or civilian. The biggest change Fran had seen was with Eva.

There was a sparkle in her eye each morning when he met her at her bedroom door, or they crossed paths on the way to the kitchen. She was relaxed, unguarded. She'd also stopped frowning and pursing her lips every time he brought a necessity or gift into the house.

The gifts were small things. He'd discovered what her favorite yogurt was, and he stocked up on two weeks' worth. He overheard her and Maggie talking about something called bath bombs. He ordered a month's worth online and stored them in the bathroom cabinet. She simply sighed when she saw them and then shut herself in the bathroom for an hour.

Fran spent that hour chatting with her brother and sister. He couldn't remember a single word that any of them had said. His mind and his entire focus were on the knob of the bathroom door where his wife was immersed in warm, sudsy, salty water.

"Look, Fran, I'm doing it."

Fran snapped his attention back to his young charge. Carlos was riding well. He'd figured out his balance quickly. He had control of the horse. The boy's self-esteem was soaring. They came back to the stables and Carlos dismounted on his own.

"Looks like you're getting your wish, soldier."

Fran turned to Dr. Patel. The man leaned on the railing as he watched Carlos. "My wish?"

"You wanted to help those kids back in Afghanistan. That's why you volunteered for the mission to build the school. Many of the inner cities of America are much like war zones."

That was the truth. The apartment complex he'd taken Eva, Carlos and Rosalee from had all the hallmarks of war; poverty, violence, firepower. Fran had saved two kids, but he thought back to the faces of the boys who'd perked up during his talk at the church. Could he save more of them? Perhaps he could try?

"I want to provide this for other children back in that neighborhood. I might not have the time to see it through. But I could get it started."

"You need to stop counting your moments and start counting your blessings," said Patel. "You have friends who literally would go to war for you. You've got these two kids who look at you like you've hung the moon. And you have a beautiful young wife who, as far as I can see, has put life back into you. Most people don't get that in a long lifetime."

Patel was right. Fran was blessed. His heart was overflowing with blessings.

"Thank you, Dr. Patel."

"For what?"

"For pushing us together."

"I'm sure I have no idea what you mean?" The man smiled with a twinkle in his eyes as he turned and headed toward the parking lot.

Fran shook his head as he watched the older man. Even before the edict came that all who chose to reside on the ranch had to be married, Patel had been pressing his case to match each of the soldiers. If Fran had listened, he might've had Eva in his life earlier. But he was happy she was there now.

She should be home soon. She'd had a late study session that evening and had taken his truck. He'd had to shove the keys into her hand and belt her into the driver's seat so she wouldn't think of taking the bus or a cab. He wanted to present her with her own car keys soon.

Fran helped Carlos put the horse up. Then the two of them collected Rosalee from the garden. They made their way to their home, the kids chattering along the way. His truck was in the driveway when they walked up to the door.

The kids pounced on their sister, regaling her of their day in school and at the ranch. Eva listened with a smile on her face as she set the table and placed a warm meal on each plate. She gazed up at Fran, brown eyes so full of warmth that his heart felt it was immersed in one of her bath bombs.

The two of them barely got a word in edgewise as the kids chattered on throughout the meal. It was Carlos's turn to clean up after dinner. But Fran took one look at the kid and his drooping eyes and sent him off to bed. Rosalee was equally as tired and hadn't argued when Eva suggested she turn in as well.

With the kids in bed and the dishes away, Fran plopped down on the sofa. A second later, Eva joined him. This had become their nightly ritual after the kids were in bed.

Eva scooted closer to Fran. He stretched his arm along the back of the couch. She immediately snuggled into the space between his shoulder cap and his breastbone. She'd claimed that spot the second night of their marriage.

Though theirs wasn't a physical relationship, he'd promised her hugs, as many as she wanted. They weren't innocent, platonic embraces and he didn't pretend they were. Fran's body was alive each time hers was near. But neither of them crossed the line of intimacy. These shared embraces were still well within the boundaries of friendship.

"How was your study session?" he asked.

"It was good."

The sound of her voice reached his heart before it reached his ears. Fran stared down at the top of Eva's head. The tendrils on the top of her head tickled his nose as he breathed in her scent. The smell of her, the feel of her supple body against his, each night it sent his heart racing.

Eva was saying more words to him, but Fran couldn't decipher them. His attention was rapt on her knees, which were resting on his thighs. She'd curled her bare feet under her bottom and her knees rested on his legs just as her head rested on his chest.

The *thump-thump* of his heart blared warning signs.

Eva laughed at something—something she'd said or something on the television, he wasn't sure. She threw back her head to look up at him. Her parted lips were a faded red, her lipstick had worn off through the day and then dinner. The muted red silenced the warning signs.

Fran couldn't take his eyes off her mouth. Her lips had stopped moving. A tremble quivered through the bottom one. She sighed and the sweetness got caught in his throat.

And still, his heart *thumped-thumped*. But the warning sounds, the warning signs, both were pointless.

Fran wasn't sure who moved first. It was likely a mutual decision. They'd been deciding so many things together the last week. It was fitting they decided this next step in their lives together.

Their lives. Together. That was the only sound he wanted to hear, the only sign he wanted to pay attention to.

This kiss was even sweeter than the sole kiss they'd shared on their wedding day. That kiss had been the taste of something new. This kiss was the promise of something familiar.

He felt his blood boiling as he drank from this woman, his wife. Fran's heartbeat raced. Faster than he knew it should. And then there was pain. A blinding pain that robbed him of his breath and wrenched him away from her.

CHAPTER EIGHTEEN

*I*t was inevitable. They both knew it. They'd been dancing around this moment for a week now.

Every night Eva came home from school. They put the kids to bed. Then they'd sit in this cocoon.

She fit so perfectly inside Fran's half embrace. The feel of his hand at her back was steadying. The divot in his shoulder had been made for her head. The sound of his heart was the sound that told her she was safe, protected, cared for.

Fran's heartbeats whispered promises. Promises that one day this easy friendship, this practical partnership, could turn into something more. Something the heart was made to do.

Everything in Eva told her that tonight that time had come.

She tilted her head back to see Fran. He looked down at her as she often caught him doing when he didn't think she was looking. For all he spoke of platonic and practicality, she knew he felt something for her. No man would go through the lengths that he'd done for her and her family without a bit of attraction.

And so when she reached up to taste his lips, she had her confirmation in his answering kiss.

Fran swept into her mouth just like he'd swept into her life. He pulled her to him, into the safety of his protection. His kiss only asked to give her pleasure. It asked nothing in return. His lips moved across hers, telling her that he just wanted to see her safe and cared for.

Eva had every plan to give this man not just her heart but her soul. It hadn't been love at first sight. It was better than that. It had been trust at first sight.

With just a glance, this man had gained her confidence. She had recognized this man was reliable and filled with integrity. Something she had found lacking in people since her parents' deaths.

Fran was able. He was strong. He was sure.

He was pulling away from her.

"Fran, I want this. I want you."

"Eva ..." He breathed hard, likely from the passion they'd shared in the all-too-brief kiss.

"Fran, I love you. I do, and I want to be your wife in every meaning of the word."

"Eva," he gasped.

He was clutching at his heart and gasping for breath. The kiss had overwhelmed her too. But not to the point of pain.

Wait.

He was clutching at his heart in pain.

His heart.

"Fran? Fran?"

But he couldn't answer. His face was contorted in agony. He gulped down deep, lungfuls of air. Just the sight of him in pain sent Eva into the throes of agony.

"What do I do? Do I call the doctor? Oh, Fran, please. I don't know what to do."

She could call 911. Or she could call out to one of the other soldiers. But she was afraid to leave him. She wiped the hair from his face. She placed her hand over his heart.

Fran gripped her hand. Slowly his eyes opened, his breathing calmed. He gazed into her eyes. She'd never seen him look so vulnerable.

It scared her.

Fran was strong, unbreakable. But in that moment, he was weak and at the mercy of an enemy he could not strike out against.

His breath steadying, he tilted his head forward to rest his face against her cheek. Eva curled her arms around his neck. She held him to her, resting his head against her own heart.

"This is why this can't happen," he said, his voice was pain-laden.

"Are you saying that kiss made your heart hurt?"

Fran lifted his head to gaze at her. His eyes were filled with regret. "It's not the kiss. It could happen at any moment. It's set off by anything, by nothing. There's no rhyme or reason to why or when the fragments in my chest move. But one day they'll get too close to my heart and kill me."

"I know," she said. She'd been doing research on his condition. She knew that fragments often moved or became encased in scar tissue.

"That could be a year from now," she said. "It could be ten years from now."

"It could be right now, Eva." He pulled away from her.

She did not let him go. "That's why I don't want to waste any more time. I want to be with you."

"Eva ..." He turned away from her, but he didn't leave from the couch.

Eva's palms came to rest over his heart. Fran clutched her hands in his, but he didn't pull away. He let out an agonized breath.

"You make my heart beat faster, Eva," he said. "But that's not what's going to kill me. What will kill me is not being here for you after, when you're hurting because of me. The idea of not being able to protect you kills me."

"Stop trying to protect me," she said. "I did just fine without you. But I do better with you. You do better with me. This may be your plan to keep me safe, but it was my choice to come here and be with you. It's my choice to stay with you. It's my plan to love you for as long as I can."

Fran hung his head. His grip on her hands loosened.

"Let me love you, Fran."

He rose from the couch. He didn't look back at her. Instead of going to his bedroom, he left out the front door.

CHAPTER NINETEEN

*E*verything hurt when Fran woke the next morning. Not just his heart. His back ached from sleeping on the hard, and at the same time lumpy, sofa. His neck spasmed from being raised high on the armrest which had elevated his head too high from the rest of his body. His left foot had fallen asleep from being exposed to the cold draft coming from the living room window.

He ran his hand over his chest. The raised scars weren't tender, hadn't been for some time. But they bothered him that morning.

Eva was fond of resting her head over that spot. She'd never come into direct contact with the scars. But every time she cuddled into him, Fran became aware of them. Even more so aware of what lay beyond them.

He wished he could reach inside his chest and pull out the fragments that kept them apart. He didn't want to jump every time his heart leaped at the sight of his wife. He didn't want to caution her against the affection he couldn't deny was growing between them. He didn't want to shut himself off from the love she'd offered up to him.

But the barrier remained. Distance was the only thing that would protect her. Perhaps he should move out of the house entirely now before the end came near.

"How'd you sleep, sunshine?"

Fran groaned at the sound of Reed's faux cheery voice. The man appeared in his bedroom door. He leaned against the frame with his good arm. The missing arm appeared as a stump in his t-shirt.

"Yeah, that's because you should be in your wife's bed," said Reed.

"It's not like that with me and Eva."

"Then you're dumber than I thought. You've got a warm-blooded, beautiful, intelligent woman who wants you. Although the fact that she wants you makes me question her intelligence. And you spent the night on my couch?"

"Getting involved with her like that, on a physical, intimate level would only hurt her more when I'm gone."

"Ah, so you'll just hurt her now. Yeah, that makes sense."

"I don't want to hurt anyone."

Reed sighed. He reached back in his room and grabbed his prosthetic. He began the process of strapping the limb on.

When the explosion had happened, Fran's first thought was to the men in his squad. Reed was closest to him. Fran had heard his cry of pain and was the first to witness his loss of limb.

He'd gone to the man, hefting Reed up and getting him to safety. Fran had been in the process of going back to look for more wounded when the pain in his chest stopped him in his tracks. He still didn't remember when the impact had happened, only its aftermath.

Fran had fallen to his knees as the cries of his friends and of the civilians whose lives he'd been trying to improve rose around him. He was paralyzed with his own pain, unable to do anything about theirs.

"A lot of the men and women I know walked into combat with a hero complex," said Reed. "You're the only one I knew who walked away a hero with a martyr complex. I don't think you can be both. You need to make a choice. Are you going to be the man who saves lives? Are you gonna be the man who dies for his beliefs?"

A knock sounded at the door. Fran closed his eyes, knowing who was on the other side. He was still raw this morning and would likely welcome Eva into his arms. Hell, he'd probably scoop her up into an embrace and not let her go, his thumping heart be damned.

More and more he wished there wasn't a wall separating them. Last night there had been whole houses between them. It wasn't far enough to escape the taste of her lips, the scent of her skin, the desire to get closer. But when the door opened, it wasn't her. It was her brother.

It was Saturday morning, so the kids hadn't had school. Fran had assumed they would sleep in. But Carlos and Rosalee had proven they loved ranch life and were up with the sun ready to get to work.

Fran lifted himself off the sofa and went out to the porch with Carlos. The two sat side by side looking out across the ranch as the sun lifted itself into the sky.

Fran knew this wasn't going to be an easygoing conversation by the strain at the edges of the kid's eyes. Neither was he sure what direction the talk would go in. So, he waited for Carlos to speak first.

"Are you guys getting a divorce?"

"No," Fran said more vehemently than he'd meant to. "When I married your sister I gave her my word. You know that a man's word is his bond."

"Yeah, but marriage is about love and you don't love her. I'm not a little kid. I don't believe in fairytales. I know there's no such thing as love at first sight."

Fran wasn't so sure. He knew it wasn't love when he first saw Eva. But he had the sense that his life had changed the moment he met her. He'd known she was meant to be in his world from that first hug at the church.

"I know you guys don't share the same bedroom." Carlos's cheeks reddened as he spoke.

Fran wasn't surprised he knew his and Eva's sleeping arrangement. Kids were nosey and Fran knew he and Eva weren't hiding that well.

"You were fighting last night," said Carlos. "I heard you raise your voices."

"It wasn't a fight. We had a disagreement."

"Isn't that another word for a fight."

Fran tried to shrug it off. "Married people fight, they disagree. It doesn't mean it's over."

"But you left."

Fran sighed. "I did. I shouldn't have."

"Why did you?"

"Because your sister wants something I can't give her. I want to give her what she wants, but I know it's not good for her. I felt like if I stayed close to her, I'd give in."

"So you ran away?"

Fran heard a chuckle from inside the house. He wanted to curse Reed. Here Fran was a decorated soldier, getting read the riot act by a kid. "Yeah. I was a coward. All right, here's the truth."

Fran looked down at the kid. Carlos looked so grown and so young at the same time. Fran knew he couldn't lie to Carlos anymore. Carlos would be the man of the house when Fran passed. Fran had to start preparing him for the responsibilities to come.

"I'm sick," said Fran.

"Sick?"

"I have a heart condition. There's shrapnel, fragments from a bomb, in my chest. They're close to my heart. They move from time to time. One day, a piece could move too close to my heart, and if it does, I'll die."

Carlos stared at Fran's chest. The kid took a deep breath. His hands balled into fists in his lap.

He was taking it far better than Fran had imagined. No tears. No whining. Just resolve.

"I knew it," Carlos finally said. "I knew I shouldn't have believed."

"Carlos?"

"You're gonna leave us just like my mom and dad."

Fran watched the kid shutter before his eyes. Fran felt trapped back in the middle of that blast in Afghanistan, needing to fight for his life so that he could save the rest of his squad. The pain was just as deep and halting. He couldn't reach Carlos.

"I knew I shouldn't have believed we could be a family forever. You're going to leave just like they did."

"Carlos—"

Fran reached for the boy, but Carlos shot out of his reach. Fran could chase him down, but to what end? The truth was the truth.

Another good deed, another life he tried to make better, and he'd only wound up hurting those he cared about. Again.

But no. Fran wouldn't let it end like that again. Carlos could still be saved. He could go after Carlos. He would do everything in his power to save the boy.

Fran leaped to his feet and ran.

CHAPTER TWENTY

*E*va had tossed and turned all night. She hadn't gotten any sleep as she lay awake waiting for any sign of Fran's return. She'd spent the time planning out exactly what she wanted to say to him.

There wasn't a single, solitary word of acquiescence in her prepared speech. No. She'd made up her mind. This marriage would be the real thing for as long as they both drew breath.

She'd even considered moving into his bedroom that morning. But in the end, felt that was a step too far.

Eva knew Fran hadn't gone far. She'd watched him walk away from her last night. He'd only made it as far as Reed's small cabin.

She hadn't gone after him. She'd given him the time to cool off, to let his heart settle, before she pounced again. In the meantime, she'd done what any good student would do. She'd begun to research.

When she couldn't sleep, she'd fired up the spare laptop Fran had; the one which hadn't ever been used before. The one that had shown up the day after her first day of class. The one she thought she'd seen the packaging for go in the trash bin. She fired it up and went straight for the internet.

The first thing her research told her was that most victims of shrapnel to the body died of their wounds in battle. That wasn't promising. Nearly every case she came across where the fragments had landed near a vital organ was fatal.

But then she found what she was looking for. There were some cases where soldiers and victims of gun violence had survived shrapnel in the chest. There were even some cases where the shrapnel moved away from the vital organs over time. Or the body put a layer of scar tissue around the fragments.

That could happen to Fran. She wanted to talk to his doctor. Or maybe they needed to go to a specialist.

It didn't matter the money. For him, she'd drop out of school, take the partial refund, and put it all into his medical bills. She'd get a minimum wage job, two if it were necessary, to pay the bills to save his life.

Just as she was planning where to look for work, the front door slammed open. Eva looked up to see her brother. His face wasn't the cheery bliss of the past week. He was angry.

"Did you know?" Carlos demanded.

"Did I know what?" Eva said, closing the laptop.

"That he was dying."

"Who's dying?" asked Rosalee coming out of her room in brand new overalls that Fran had snuck into her room the other day. Rosie looked like a little farm girl.

Looking back over at her brother, Eva sighed. She'd spent years comforting her brother and sister after their father's death, during their mother's illness, from her relatives' inconsistencies and unreliability, from the violence of the neighborhoods they had no choice but to live in. This was something she couldn't hide from them.

"He's not dying," Eva said. "He has metal fragments in his chest."

"That could kill him at any minute." Carlos crossed his arms over his chest and glared. It was the same face he'd made as an adolescent when

Eva tried to get him to eat his peas. His mind was set.

"Yes," she conceded. "But he could also live a long and happy life."

"Fran has something wrong with his heart?" said Rosalee, her voice tremored and her eyes grew large like empty saucers.

The door opened again, and the man in question walked in. Fran's gaze immediately tracked to Eva's. There was an apology, shame, worry, and wariness all rolled into one there.

He was out of breath. Heaving lungfuls of air. He doubled over at the threshold of the door.

Eva and her siblings looked at him. Eyes wide, mouths agape. No one moved as they watched him gulp down air. Rosalee began to wail. Carlos balled and unballed his fists.

Fran raised his head to her. That set her in motion.

Eva had him in her arms, taking the brunt of his large body with hers and urging him to the sofa. His gaze was so soft when it met hers.

"I'm sorry," he said. His voice was quiet as he labored to breathe. "I should not have walked out on you last night. It was cowardly. Please forgive me."

"You're forgiven. Please just try to calm down. Take deep breaths. You're going to be fine."

Fran tore his gaze away from her and found Carlos. Carlos came to him, sitting at his right side. "Men don't run from their responsibilities. We're family forever."

Carlos nodded, clasping Fran's hand. Tears burned at the corners of his eyes. The struggle to keep them in check was evident.

Fran turned his gaze to Rosalee. "Hey, princess."

"Please don't die, Fran," Rosalee wailed.

"I'm gonna try my hardest, okay?"

"Okay." Rosalee nodded.

Fran turned back to Eva. "Hey."

"Hey."

"I need you to call my doctor."

CHAPTER TWENTY-ONE

The pain was so intense that Fran couldn't speak. Eva leaned over him, concern etched on her pretty face. He lifted a hand, aiming to touch her cheek, to smooth away her worry. But his limbs shook with the effort.

He hadn't wanted to give up, not on his efforts to reach out to her, not on his desire to stay with her, to be with her for the rest of his life, however long that might be. But his body wouldn't cooperate.

Eva reached down to his trembling fingers. She curled them in her own. Lifting his knuckles to her lips, she pressed a kiss to each joint.

Fran felt her whisper into his palm. He felt the formation of the word *love* as her lips skimmed his palm. Her tongue rose to the roof of her mouth to make the L sound. He felt the burst of staccato breath that would make the ST sound and had to imagine she was begging him to stay.

He wanted nothing more. He wanted to be her hero. He wanted to be the man who raised a weapon to defend her. The man who went into danger to gather her sustenance. The man who wrapped her into his arms, not only for protection but for comfort. He wanted to be her everything. He didn't want to die to have to do it.

The moment she'd said that she would marry him, Fran had buried himself in a mountain of paperwork. He signed everything over to her in the event of his death. She and her siblings would never want for anything for the rest of their lives.

But he'd gotten that wrong. They'd only ever wanted him.

As the gurney wheeled around a corner, Fran caught his last glimpse of Carlos and Rosalee. Carlos's stiff upper lip quivered as distance increased between himself and Fran. The young man wrapped an arm around his little sister's shoulder. Rosalee was a fountain of tears. Her hand reached out to Fran, but he was beyond her now.

Fran wanted to scoop the little thing into his arms and tell her he'd be back. That he'd be there for her. More than anything, he wanted to be there for them all. He hadn't wanted his death to be what saved them. He wanted to live for them.

He hadn't wanted to die a martyr. He wanted to live as their hero.

All around him doctors swarmed in. They parted Eva from him.

"I'm his wife," she insisted.

But her status didn't get her access to the operating room. A woman in a nurse's uniform barred Eva's entry. Reed put an arm around her waist and pulled her close as they wheeled Fran away.

Eva's body sank into Reed's. Her gaze never left Fran. He saw her eyes brim with worry and fear. Before the door's closed, her lips lifted in the smallest of smiles.

He knew it took a great effort for that smile. He could nearly read her mind. If this was going to be the last time he saw her, he wanted it to be with her smiling.

That woman. Thinking of everyone else even to the end.

Fran fought the pain that centered in his chest. It robbed him of his breath. He couldn't speak to her, he couldn't tell her the words he needed to say, the most important thing he ever had to say.

He couldn't shout the words, but he moved his lips to communicate the message.

The effort robbed him of his last bit of strength. The second the last of the three words were formed, he collapsed back down onto the gurney. And his world turned to black.

CHAPTER TWENTY-TWO

*T*he waiting room at the hospital was packed. Dylan held a sleeping Maggie on his lap. Reed held a sleeping Rosalee on his lap. Rosie rested her head against Reed's prosthetic arm as he stroked her back with his other hand. Sean and Xavier took turns pacing the small space. Eva sat with her eyes glued to the door where she'd seen the doctors exit to talk with the family of the patients.

That door had opened three times in the last two hours. She'd overheard three conversations. Two of them had induced tears from the family. And not happy tears. Only one had brought on sighs of relief.

There were no other families in the waiting area now. Eva hoped the odds were in her family's favor that when the doors opened again, they'd be delivering sighs of relief. But the doors hadn't swung open in over forty-five minutes.

There was silence amongst the guys. No one offered her consoling words. They all knew the chances were that when the doors opened the next time, there would unlikely be any sighs of relief.

But they hadn't left her side. They'd surrounded her and her family, insulating them as best they could.

Carlos sat next to her, his eyes on the door just as hers had been for the last hour.

Eva opened her mouth to offer her brother consolation. But the words stuck in her throat.

Carlos turned to her. Her baby brother looked so old at the moment.

"I think we should pray," he said.

Eva blinked. Those were the last words she'd expected to hear from him.

"I was angry at God for a long time," Carlos continued. "I thought he'd forgotten about us when he took Mom and Dad. Then he sent us Fran. I never said thank you."

Carlos bent his head. After a moment, the others followed suit.

"Dear God, thank you for bringing Fran to my family. He taught me what I need to know to be a man. That a man takes care of his family. Moms and sisters do that too. Family takes care of family. I promise to do that from now on. If you have to take Fran tonight, please introduce him to my mom and dad so that they can take care of him the way he took care of us. Amen."

"Amen," their new family intoned.

A swishing sound brought all of their attention around. There was a man in a white coat standing in the doorway. The look on the doctor's face was grave.

The men rose. As a unit they moved in closer to Eva, standing at her side, at her back. Eva knew that no matter the news, whether tears or sighs, Fran had given her his love. He'd given her a family that would always have her back and never leave her alone. Still, she wished to have him at her back.

A tear slid down her cheek as the doctor opened his mouth to deliver the news.

CHAPTER TWENTY-THREE

A bright light shone on the other side of Fran's eyelids. He kept his eyes shut, not wanting to wake from the dream he'd been having. In the dream, he was sitting and talking with an elderly husband and wife. He knew the conversation had been long and pleasant. But at the moment, Fran couldn't recall a single word they'd exchanged.

What he did hold onto was the warm feeling in his heart, the smile of the wife, the look of approval the husband gave him. As they waved him off, Fran felt somehow empowered to take on the world.

But he still wasn't ready to wake up. So he stayed in the dream. In the blink of an eye, Eva was there. She stood in the sun, in a dress similar to the one she'd worn on their wedding day.

Fran walked up behind her. He slid his arms around her and pulled her body back into his. She was safe and content inside his arms. She tilted her face up, and he leaned down and kissed her.

Sunshine dawned in his heart. Rays of warmth spread as he sipped her in. He pressed her closer to him.

The light from the other side grew brighter, insisting he wake. Then Fran realized something; he could wake.

He wasn't dead. He was alive. That meant he could have Eva in the flesh.

He let go of his dream, and his eyes sprang open. It took a moment for his vision to adjust. When it did, he saw warm brown eyes gazing down at him. They weren't Eva's.

"You're gonna be okay," said Carlos. "I prayed for you. We all did."

Fran spied movement beyond the door. He caught sight of his squad. Their heads were turned, speaking to a man in a white coat. Reed caught Fran's eye from the other side of the glass. His friend winked.

"They said only two people in the room at a time," said Carlos.

Two people? Fran's gaze slid around. He spied

Eva in a chair against the wall. Her eyes were closed, but he saw signs of stirring.

"She's been here all night. We've been taking turns coming in and sitting with you."

Fran couldn't take his eyes off his wife. He watched as her eyes fluttered open. They were hazy at first. When her gaze met his, the fog cleared, and she sat up.

"I took care of them all while you were asleep," Carlos continued. "I stayed by their side like a man does for his family."

Fran looked back at the young man. He lifted his hand and placed it on his cheek. "You did good."

Carlos nodded in agreement. Then he slid off the bed. He gave his sister a hug, and then he slipped out the door.

Eva made her way to Fran on slow feet. Fran wanted to sit up, to get up, to get to her faster. He reached his hand out to her. She took his fingers and sat down on the bed next to him.

"I'm sorry," he said.

"It's okay. You're okay."

"I promise you, I won't ever push you away like that again. I love you, Eva. I want us to be together, in a real marriage. I want to hold you. I want to kiss you. I want to fall asleep and wake up with you in my arms. If I only have another hour, I want to spend that time with you."

Fran brushed away a tear from her eye. She turned her face into his palm and kissed it.

"I love you, Fran. We're going to have more than an hour together. We're going to have a lifetime."

He'd let her believe that. He'd take every moment and treasure it.

"The shrapnel," she said. "It moved away from your heart. I don't really understand it all, but the doctor said that where it's moving, it'll likely form scar tissue that will hold it still."

Fran struggled to understand her words. They were too good to be true.

"They said you might feel more pain from time to time," she continued. "But the fragments are moving in a positive direction."

Fran wanted to laugh. He'd suffer an ache in his chest from time to time if it meant he got to have this love. Not just Eva's love, but the love of his entire family. He spied them all watching with grins on their faces from the doorway.

They all let out a cheer now that he knew the prognosis. Eva laughed. Fran did too.

He'd set out to save this woman and her family, to move them out of a danger zone and into safety.

He hadn't expected them all to steal his heart and save his life. Now they had, the dangerous bits inside him had given way. Fran followed suit.

He turned to her, tugging her closer. Their lips met. It was nothing like the dream he'd just had. It was so much more because it was real, because this kiss, this love, this family, it would last.

EPILOGUE

Reed kept his eye on the bouncing ball as Xavier danced around the basketball hoop at the head of the driveway. He remained light on his feet as Xavier danced around, dribbling between his legs more like a backup dancer than a baller. Reed paid the performance no mind. He knew it would only be a matter of moments before his shot came.

He gave his shoulders a shake. Clenching and releasing the fingers of his sole hand, he lay in wait, ready to grab for his chance and steal the game-winning point. No one watching the game would think to consider that he had a lesser chance of winning due to the fact that he had only one fully functioning arm in a game where handling the ball was key. He and Xavier weren't evenly matched at all. Reed had the upper hand.

Watching his friend continue his fancy footwork, Reed kept calm and gathered the facts. That's all he'd need to turn the game to his advantage. His careful observations quickly panned out.

Xavier favored his left side. He kept the ball in his left hand more times than not. When he went for the shot, it would be with his right hand.

Reed squared up against his friend. Xavier faked a jab to his left. Reed hadn't fallen for it. Reed attacked, using the stump of his special arm. With Xavier being on his subordinate side, it was easy to knock the ball out of his left hand.

Once the ball was free of Xavier's grasp, Reed stepped in. Using his body to block Xavier, Reed grabbed the ball with his own left hand. He pivoted his body, turning toward the hoop and made the shot.

The swish of the corded rope was louder than the applause of an NBA stadium at playoffs. But it was Xavier's groan that was music to Reed's ears.

"You've gotta be kidding me," groaned Xavier.

"Don't hate the player," said Reed.

"Let's go again. Best three out of five."

Xavier was a sore loser. But Reed was feeling

pretty sore after two full out games. Before he could decline, the sound of a truck pulling up pushed the two men out of the driveway and into the yard. Once the truck was in park, Fran opened the passenger side door and stepped out.

Reed stepped up to the driver's side to hand out Eva. Eva smiled, grateful as she took his hand and hopped down to the ground.

"DeMonti," called Xavier, "think fast."

The basketball sailed through the air. Fran reached out his hands, but Eva smacked the ball away. Those same quick hands went to her hips, and her gaze shot balls of fury at Xavier. Reed's brows raised in shock. How in the heck had she gotten around the car that fast?

"Xavier Hunter Ramos if you over-excite my husband, I will tan your hide," Eva said.

Xavier straightened his back like the soldier he was. His shoulders snapped to attention and his head tilted as though he'd received an order from a commanding officer.

Reed's body reacted in the same manner. His right hand itched to rise to a salute.

"Are we clear?" Eva said to Xavier. Behind her Fran smirked at his friend.

"Ma'am, yes, ma'am," said Xavier.

"He is to have no excitement for the next few weeks," Eva said wrapping her arms around Fran's torso and placing her hand on his heart.

Now it was Xavier who smirked at Fran. Fran had been married for two weeks and there had been no excitement in his marital bed. Unlike Xavier who went out to get his kicks every weekend with a different girl.

"Come on, let's get you into bed," said Eva.

"Ma'am, yes, ma'am," grinned Fran.

"To rest," said Eva. "The doctor said you need to take it easy, Fran."

Fran hadn't argued. He'd placed a light kiss at his wife's lips and allowed her to lead him inside the house.

Reed watched after them. Soon that would be him.

The dating app had found him a woman with a compatibility rating of ninety-eight percent. Sarai Austin was perfect on paper. And soon they'd meet in real life, once she got back into the country from her overseas business trip.

Reed had chatted with Sarai online every day since they'd connected through the app. The more he spoke to her, the more he knew she was the one for him. He just needed to meet her in person to seal the deal. But for the second week straight, she'd been called out of town for business.

He admired her dedication to her job. And he was a patient man. But there was a deadline he was up against. The edict that he had to get married in just under two months. Reed just knew that if they could meet in person, everything would align. The data told him so.

The two of them had so much in common, and their conversations were so easy he'd swear he'd known her for years and not days. She'd seen his injury. He'd displayed images of him sleeveless with his stump, and his arm with a prosthetic prominently on his profile. She'd said she wasn't averse to it, and he believed her.

He just needed to look in her eyes. Then, just like Dylan and Fran, he'd have a woman who'd place her hand over his heart and fiercely protect that organ with all that she was. He'd have a woman tilt her head back, offering her lips to him for a kiss. He'd have a woman he'd wrap his arms around, a woman who knew his love was true and whole. Even if he couldn't quite lock her in an embrace, she'd never doubt that he'd hold her.

The moment Sarai touched down back on US soil, he'd have it all.

Soon ...

Wanna know a secret?
Sarai's not out of the country.
She's actually not far from the ranch.
It's just she has a little—well, big secret that she's not
sure Reed will be able to accept.
Wanna know what it is?

You'll find out soon enough in
"Offering His Arm"
the third book in The Brides of Purple Heart Ranch!

Shanae Johnson was raised by Saturday Morning cartoons and After School Specials. She still doesn't understand why there isn't a life lesson that ties the issues of the day together just before bedtime. While she's still waiting for the meaning of it all, she writes stories to try and figure it all out. Her books are wholesome and sweet, but her are heroes are hot and heroines are full of sass!

And by the way, the E elongates the A. So it's pronounced Shan-aaaaaaaa. Perfect for a hero to call out across the moors, or up to a balcony, or to blare outside her window on a boombox. If you hear him calling her name, please send him her way!

You can sign up for Shanae's Reader Group at

http://bit.ly/ShanaeJohnsonReaders

Also By Shanae Johnson

The Brides of Purple Heart

On His Bended Knee

Hand Over His Heart

The Marquis and the Magician's Assistant

The Princess and the Principal

Made in the USA
Coppell, TX
31 October 2022

85488637R00098